The Duchesse of Langeais

Honoré de Balzac

Translated by Ellen Marriage

THE DUCHESSE OF LANGEAIS

By Honore De Balzac

Translated by Ellen Marriage

To Franz Liszt

THE DUCHESSE OF LANGEAIS

In a Spanish city on an island in the Mediterranean, there stands a convent of the Order of Barefoot Carmelites, where the rule instituted by St. Theresa is still preserved with all the first rigor of the reformation brought about by that illustrious woman. Extraordinary as this may seem, it is none the less true. Almost every religious house in the Peninsula, or in Europe for that matter, was either destroyed or disorganized by the outbreak of the French Revolution and the Napoleonic wars; but as this island was protected through those times by the English fleet, its wealthy convent and peaceable inhabitants were secure from the general trouble and spoliation. The storms of many kinds which shook the first fifteen years of the nineteenth century spent their force before they reached those cliffs at so short a distance from the coast of Andalusia.

If the rumour of the Emperor's name so much as reached the shore of the island, it is doubtful whether the holy women kneeling in the cloisters grasped the reality of his dream-like progress of glory, or the majesty that blazed in flame across kingdom after kingdom during his meteor life.

In the minds of the Roman Catholic world, the convent stood out pre-eminent for a stern discipline which nothing had changed; the purity of its rule had attracted unhappy women from the furthest parts of Europe, women deprived of all human ties, sighing after the long suicide accomplished in the breast of God. No convent, indeed, was so well fitted for that complete detachment of the soul from all earthly things, which is demanded by the religious life, albeit on the continent of Europe there are many convents magnificently adapted to the purpose of their existence. Buried away in the loneliest valleys, hanging in mid-air on the steepest mountainsides, set down on the brink of precipices, in every place man has sought for the poetry of the Infinite, the solemn awe of Silence; in every place man has striven to draw closer to God, seeking Him on mountain peaks, in the depths below the crags, at the cliff's edge; and everywhere man has found God. But nowhere, save on this half-European, half-

1

African ledge of rock could you find so many different harmonies, combining so to raise the soul, that the sharpest pain comes to be like other memories; the strongest impressions are dulled, till the sorrows of life are laid to rest in the depths.

The convent stands on the highest point of the crags at the uttermost end of the island. On the side towards the sea the rock was once rent sheer away in some globe-cataclysm; it rises up a straight wall from the base where the waves gnaw at the stone below high-water mark. Any assault is made impossible by the dangerous reefs that stretch far out to sea, with the sparkling waves of the Mediterranean playing over them. So, only from the sea can you discern the square mass of the convent built conformably to the minute rules laid down as to the shape, height, doors, and windows of monastic buildings. From the side of the town, the church completely hides the solid structure of the cloisters and their roofs, covered with broad slabs of stone impervious to sun or storm or gales of wind.

The church itself, built by the munificence of a Spanish family, is the crowning edifice of the town. Its fine, bold front gives an imposing and picturesque look to the little city in the sea. The sight of such a city, with its close-huddled roofs, arranged for the most part amphitheatre-wise above a picturesque harbour, and crowned by a glorious cathedral front with triple-arched Gothic doorways, belfry towers, and filigree spires, is a spectacle surely in every way the sublimest on earth. Religion towering above daily life, to put men continually in mind of the End and the way, is in truth a thoroughly Spanish conception. But now surround this picture by the Mediterranean, and a burning sky, imagine a few palms here and there, a few stunted evergreen trees mingling their waving leaves with the motionless flowers and foliage of carved stone; look out over the reef with its white fringes of foam in contrast to the sapphire sea; and then turn to the city, with its galleries and terraces whither the townsfolk come to take the air among their flowers of an evening, above the houses and the tops of the trees in their little gardens; add a few sails down in the harbour; and lastly, in the stillness of falling night, listen to the organ music, the chanting of the services, the wonderful sound of bells pealing out over the open sea.

There is sound and silence everywhere; oftener still there is silence over all.

The church is divided within into a sombre mysterious nave and narrow aisles. For some reason, probably because the winds are so high, the architect was unable to build the flying buttresses and intervening chapels which adorn almost all cathedrals, nor are there openings of any kind in the walls which support the weight of the roof. Outside there is simply the heavy wall structure, a solid mass of grey stone further strengthened by huge piers placed at intervals. Inside, the nave and its little side galleries are lighted entirely by the great stained-glass rose-window suspended by a miracle of art above the centre doorway; for upon that side the exposure permits of the display of lacework in stone and of other beauties peculiar to the style improperly called Gothic.

The larger part of the nave and aisles was left for the townsfolk, who came and went and heard mass there. The choir was shut off from the rest of the church by a grating and thick folds of brown curtain, left slightly apart in the middle in such a way that nothing of the choir could be seen from the church except the high altar and the officiating priest. The grating itself was divided up by the pillars which supported the organ loft; and this part of the structure, with its carved wooden columns, completed the line of the arcading in the gallery carried by the shafts in the nave. If any inquisitive person, therefore, had been bold enough to climb upon the narrow balustrade in the gallery to look down into the choir, he could have seen nothing but the tall eight-sided windows of stained glass beyond the high altar.

At the time of the French expedition into Spain to establish Ferdinand VII once more on the throne, a French general came to the island after the taking of Cadiz, ostensibly to require the recognition of the King's Government, really to see the convent and to find some means of entering it. The undertaking was certainly a delicate one; but a man of passionate temper, whose life had been, as it were, but one series of poems in action, a man who all his life long had lived romances instead of writing them, a man pre-eminently a Doer, was sure to be tempted by a deed which seemed to be impossible.

3

To open the doors of a convent of nuns by lawful means! The metropolitan or the Pope would scarcely have permitted it! And as for force or stratagem—might not any indiscretion cost him his position, his whole career as a soldier, and the end in view to boot? The Duc d'Angouleme was still in Spain; and of all the crimes which a man in favour with the Commander-in-Chief might commit, this one alone was certain to find him inexorable. The General had asked for the mission to gratify private motives of curiosity, though never was curiosity more hopeless. This final attempt was a matter of conscience. The Carmelite convent on the island was the only nunnery in Spain which had baffled his search.

As he crossed from the mainland, scarcely an hour's distance, he felt a presentiment that his hopes were to be fulfilled; and afterwards, when as yet he had seen nothing of the convent but its walls, and of the nuns not so much as their robes; while he had merely heard the chanting of the service, there were dim auguries under the walls and in the sound of the voices to justify his frail hope. And, indeed, however faint those so unaccountable presentiments might be, never was human passion more vehemently excited than the General's curiosity at that moment. There are no small events for the heart; the heart exaggerates everything; the heart weighs the fall of a fourteen-year-old Empire and the dropping of a woman's glove in the same scales, and the glove is nearly always the heavier of the two. So here are the facts in all their prosaic simplicity. The facts first, the emotions will follow.

An hour after the General landed on the island, the royal authority was re-established there. Some few Constitutional Spaniards who had found their way thither after the fall of Cadiz were allowed to charter a vessel and sail for London. So there was neither resistance nor reaction. But the change of government could not be effected in the little town without a mass, at which the two divisions under the General's command were obliged to be present. Now, it was upon this mass that the General had built his hopes of gaining some information as to the sisters in the convent; he was quite unaware how absolutely the Carmelites were cut off from the world; but he knew that there might be among them one whom he held dearer than life, dearer than honour.

His hopes were cruelly dashed at once. Mass, it is true, was celebrated in state. In honour of such a solemnity, the curtains which always hid the choir were drawn back to display its riches, its valuable paintings and shrines so bright with gems that they eclipsed the glories of the ex-votos of gold and silver hung up by sailors of the port on the columns in the nave. But all the nuns had taken refuge in the organ-loft. And yet, in spite of this first check, during this very mass of thanksgiving, the most intimately thrilling drama that ever set a man's heart beating opened out widely before him.

The sister who played the organ aroused such intense enthusiasm, that not a single man regretted that he had come to the service. Even the men in the ranks were delighted, and the officers were in ecstasy. As for the General, he was seemingly calm and indifferent. The sensations stirred in him as the sister played one piece after another belong to the small number of things which it is not lawful to utter; words are powerless to express them; like death, God, eternity, they can only be realised through their one point of contact with humanity. Strangely enough, the organ music seemed to belong to the school of Rossini, the musician who brings most human passion into his art.

Some day his works, by their number and extent, will receive the reverence due to the Homer of music. From among all the scores that we owe to his great genius, the nun seemed to have chosen *Moses in Egypt* for special study, doubtless because the spirit of sacred music finds therein its supreme expression. Perhaps the soul of the great musician, so gloriously known to Europe, and the soul of this unknown executant had met in the intuitive apprehension of the same poetry. So at least thought two dilettanti officers who must have missed the Theatre Favart in Spain.

At last in the *Te Deum* no one could fail to discern a French soul in the sudden change that came over the music. Joy for the victory of the Most Christian King evidently stirred this nun's heart to the depths. She was a Frenchwoman beyond mistake. Soon the love of country shone out, breaking forth like shafts of light from the fugue, as the sister introduced variations with all a Parisienne's fastidious taste, and blended vague suggestions of our grandest national airs

5

with her music. A Spaniard's fingers would not have brought this warmth into a graceful tribute paid to the victorious arms of France. The musician's nationality was revealed.

"We find France everywhere, it seems," said one of the men.

The General had left the church during the *Te Deum*; he could not listen any longer. The nun's music had been a revelation of a woman loved to frenzy; a woman so carefully hidden from the world's eyes, so deeply buried in the bosom of the Church, that hitherto the most ingenious and persistent efforts made by men who brought great influence and unusual powers to bear upon the search had failed to find her. The suspicion aroused in the General's heart became all but a certainty with the vague reminiscence of a sad, delicious melody, the air of *Fleuve du Tage*. The woman he loved had played the prelude to the ballad in a boudoir in Paris, how often! and now this nun had chosen the song to express an exile's longing, amid the joy of those that triumphed. Terrible sensation! To hope for the resurrection of a lost love, to find her only to know that she was lost, to catch a mysterious glimpse of her after five years—five years, in which the pent-up passion, chafing in an empty life, had grown the mightier for every fruitless effort to satisfy it!

Who has not known, at least once in his life, what it is to lose some precious thing; and after hunting through his papers, ransacking his memory, and turning his house upside down; after one or two days spent in vain search, and hope, and despair; after a prodigious expenditure of the liveliest irritation of soul, who has not known the ineffable pleasure of finding that all-important nothing which had come to be a king of monomania? Very good. Now, spread that fury of search over five years; put a woman, put a heart, put love in the place of the trifle; transpose the monomania into the key of high passion; and, furthermore, let the seeker be a man of ardent temper, with a lion's heart and a leonine head and mane, a man to inspire awe and fear in those who come in contact with him—realise this, and you may, perhaps, understand why the General walked abruptly out of the church when the first notes of a ballad, which he used to hear with a rapture of delight in a gilt-paneled boudoir, began to vibrate along the aisles of the church in the sea.

6

The General walked away down the steep street which led to the port, and only stopped when he could not hear the deep notes of the organ. Unable to think of anything but the love which broke out in volcanic eruption, filling his heart with fire, he only knew that the *Te Deum* was over when the Spanish congregation came pouring out of the church. Feeling that his behaviour and attitude might seem ridiculous, he went back to head the procession, telling the alcalde and the governor that, feeling suddenly faint, he had gone out into the air. Casting about for a plea for prolonging his stay, it at once occurred to him to make the most of this excuse, framed on the spur of the moment. He declined, on a plea of increasing indisposition, to preside at the banquet given by the town to the French officers, betook himself to his bed, and sent a message to the Major-General, to the effect that temporary illness obliged him to leave the Colonel in command of the troops for the time being. This commonplace but very plausible stratagem relieved him of all responsibility for the time necessary to carry out his plans. The General, nothing if not "catholic and monarchical," took occasion to inform himself of the hours of the services, and manifested the greatest zeal for the performance of his religious duties, piety which caused no remark in Spain.

The very next day, while the division was marching out of the town, the General went to the convent to be present at vespers. He found an empty church. The townsfolk, devout though they were, had all gone down to the quay to watch the embarkation of the troops. He felt glad to be the only man there. He tramped noisily up the nave, clanking his spurs till the vaulted roof rang with the sound; he coughed, he talked aloud to himself to let the nuns know, and more particularly to let the organist know that if the troops were gone, one Frenchman was left behind. Was this singular warning heard and understood? He thought so. It seemed to him that in the *Magnificat* the organ made response which was borne to him on the vibrating air. The nun's spirit found wings in music and fled towards him, throbbing with the rhythmical pulse of the sounds. Then, in all its might, the music burst forth and filled the church with warmth. The Song of Joy set apart in the sublime liturgy of Latin Christianity to express the exaltation of the soul in the presence of the glory of the ever-living God, became the utterance of a heart almost terrified by its gladness in the presence of the glory of a mortal love; a love that yet lived, a love that had risen to trouble her even beyond the grave in which the nun is laid, that she may rise again as the bride of Christ.

The organ is in truth the grandest, the most daring, the most magnificent of all instruments invented by human genius. It is a whole orchestra in itself. It can express anything in response to a skilled touch. Surely it is in some sort a pedestal on which the soul poises for a flight forth into space, essaying on her course to draw picture after picture in an endless series, to paint human life, to cross the Infinite that separates heaven from earth? And the longer a dreamer listens to those giant harmonies, the better he realizes that nothing save this hundred-voiced choir on earth can fill all the space between kneeling men, and a God hidden by the blinding light of the Sanctuary. The music is the one interpreter strong enough to bear up the prayers of humanity to heaven, prayer in its omnipotent moods, prayer tinged by the melancholy of many different natures, coloured by meditative ecstasy, upspringing with the impulse of repentance — blended with the myriad fancies of every creed. Yes. In those long vaulted aisles the melodies inspired by the sense of things divine are blended with a grandeur unknown before, are decked with new glory and might. Out of the dim daylight, and the deep silence broken by the chanting of the choir in response to the thunder of the organ, a veil is woven for God, and the brightness of His attributes shines through it.

And this wealth of holy things seemed to be flung down like a grain of incense upon the fragile altar raised to Love beneath the eternal throne of a jealous and avenging God. Indeed, in the joy of the nun there was little of that awe and gravity which should harmonize with the solemnities of the *Magnificat*. She had enriched the music with graceful variations, earthly gladness throbbing through the rhythm of each. In such brilliant quivering notes some great singer might strive to find a voice for her love, her melodies fluttered as a bird flutters about her mate. There were moments when she seemed to leap back into the past, to dally there now with laughter, now with tears. Her changing moods, as it were, ran riot. She was like a woman excited and happy over her lover's return.

But at length, after the swaying fugues of delirium, after the marvellous rendering of a vision of the past, a revulsion swept over the soul that thus found utterance for itself. With a swift transition from the major to the minor, the organist told her hearer of her present lot. She gave the story of long melancholy broodings, of the slow course of her moral malady. How day by day she deadened the senses, how every night cut off one more thought, how her heart was slowly reduced to ashes. The sadness deepened shade after shade through languid modulations, and in a little while the echoes were pouring out a torrent of grief. Then on a sudden, high notes rang out like the voices of angels singing together, as if to tell the lost but not forgotten lover that their spirits now could only meet in heaven. Pathetic hope! Then followed the *Amen*. No more joy, no more tears in the air, no sadness, no regrets. The *Amen* was the return to God. The final chord was deep, solemn, even terrible; for the last rumblings of the bass sent a shiver through the audience that raised the hair on their heads; the nun shook out her veiling of crepe, and seemed to sink again into the grave from which she had risen for a moment. Slowly the reverberations died away; it seemed as if the church, but now so full of light, had returned to thick darkness.

The General had been caught up and borne swiftly away by this strong-winged spirit; he had followed the course of its flight from beginning to end. He understood to the fullest extent the imagery of that burning symphony; for him the chords reached deep and far. For him, as for the sister, the poem meant future, present, and past. Is not music, and even opera music, a sort of text, which a susceptible or poetic temper, or a sore and stricken heart, may expand as memories shall determine? If a musician must needs have the heart of a poet, must not the listener too be in a manner a poet and a lover to hear all that lies in great music? Religion, love, and music—what are they but a threefold expression of the same fact, of that craving for expansion which stirs in every noble soul. And these three forms of poetry ascend to God, in whom all passion on earth finds its end. Wherefore the holy human trinity finds a place amid the infinite glories of God; of God, whom we always represent surrounded with the fires of love and seistrons of gold—music and light and harmony. Is not He the Cause and the End of all our strivings?

The French General guessed rightly that here in the desert, on this bare rock in the sea, the nun had seized upon music as an outpouring of the passion that still consumed her. Was this her manner of offering up her love as a sacrifice to God? Or was it Love exultant in triumph over God? The questions were hard to answer. But one thing at least the General could not mistake—in this heart, dead to the world, the fire of passion burned as fiercely as in his own.

Vespers over, he went back to the alcalde with whom he was staying. In the all-absorbing joy which comes in such full measure when a satisfaction sought long and painfully is attained at last, he could see nothing beyond this—he was still loved! In her heart love had grown in loneliness, even as his love had grown stronger as he surmounted one barrier after another which this woman had set between them! The glow of soul came to its natural end. There followed a longing to see her again, to contend with God for her, to snatch her away—a rash scheme, which appealed to a daring nature. He went to bed, when the meal was over, to avoid questions; to be alone and think at his ease; and he lay absorbed by deep thought till day broke.

He rose only to go to mass. He went to the church and knelt close to the screen, with his forehead touching the curtain; he would have torn a hole in it if he had been alone, but his host had come with him out of politeness, and the least imprudence might compromise the whole future of his love, and ruin the new hopes.

The organ sounded, but it was another player, and not the nun of the last two days whose hands touched the keys. It was all colorless and cold for the General. Was the woman he loved prostrated by emotion which well-nigh overcame a strong man's heart? Had she so fully realised and shared an unchanged, longed-for love, that now she lay dying on her bed in her cell? While innumerable thoughts of this kind perplexed his mind, the voice of the woman he worshipped rang out close beside him; he knew its clear resonant soprano. It was her voice, with that faint tremor in it which gave it all the charm that shyness and diffidence gives to a young girl; her voice, distinct from the mass of singing as a *prima donna's* in the chorus of a finale. It was like a golden or silver thread in dark frieze.

10

It was she! There could be no mistake. Parisienne now as ever, she had not laid coquetry aside when she threw off worldly adornments for the veil and the Carmelite's coarse serge. She who had affirmed her love last evening in the praise sent up to God, seemed now to say to her lover, "Yes, it is I. I am here. My love is unchanged, but I am beyond the reach of love. You will hear my voice, my soul shall enfold you, and I shall abide here under the brown shroud in the choir from which no power on earth can tear me. You shall never see me more!"

"It is she indeed!" the General said to himself, raising his head. He had leant his face on his hands, unable at first to bear the intolerable emotion that surged like a whirlpool in his heart, when that well-known voice vibrated under the arcading, with the sound of the sea for accompaniment.

Storm was without, and calm within the sanctuary. Still that rich voice poured out all its caressing notes; it fell like balm on the lover's burning heart; it blossomed upon the air—the air that a man would fain breathe more deeply to receive the effluence of a soul breathed forth with love in the words of the prayer. The alcalde coming to join his guest found him in tears during the elevation, while the nun was singing, and brought him back to his house. Surprised to find so much piety in a French military man, the worthy magistrate invited the confessor of the convent to meet his guest. Never had news given the General more pleasure; he paid the ecclesiastic a good deal of attention at supper, and confirmed his Spanish hosts in the high opinion they had formed of his piety by a not wholly disinterested respect.

He inquired with gravity how many sisters there were in the convent, and asked for particulars of its endowment and revenues, as if from courtesy he wished to hear the good priest discourse on the subject most interesting to him. He informed himself as to the manner of life led by the holy women. Were they allowed to go out of the convent, or to see visitors?

"Senor," replied the venerable churchman, "the rule is strict. A woman cannot enter a monastery of the order of St. Bruno without a special permission from His Holiness, and the rule here is equally stringent. No man may enter a convent of Barefoot Carmelites unless he is a priest specially attached to the services of the house by the Archbishop. None of the nuns may leave the convent; though the great Saint, St. Theresa, often left her cell. The Visitor or the Mothers Superior can alone give permission, subject to an authorization from the Archbishop, for a nun to see a visitor, and then especially in a case of illness. Now we are one of the principal houses, and consequently we have a Mother Superior here. Among other foreign sisters there is one Frenchwoman, Sister Theresa; she it is who directs the music in the chapel."

"Oh!" said the General, with feigned surprise. "She must have rejoiced over the victory of the House of Bourbon."

"I told them the reason of the mass; they are always a little bit inquisitive."

"But Sister Theresa may have interests in France. Perhaps she would like to send some message or to hear news."

"I do not think so. She would have come to ask me."

"As a fellow-countryman, I should be quite curious to see her," said the General. "If it is possible, if the Lady Superior consents, if — —"

"Even at the grating and in the Reverend Mother's presence, an interview would be quite impossible for anybody whatsoever; but, strict as the Mother is, for a deliverer of our holy religion and the throne of his Catholic Majesty, the rule might be relaxed for a moment," said the confessor, blinking. "I will speak about it."

"How old is Sister Theresa?" inquired the lover. He dared not ask any questions of the priest as to the nun's beauty.

"She does not reckon years now," the good man answered, with a simplicity that made the General shudder.

Next day before siesta, the confessor came to inform the French General that Sister Theresa and the Mother consented to receive him at the grating in the parlour before vespers. The General spent the siesta in pacing to and fro along the quay in the noonday heat. Thither the priest came to find him, and brought him to the convent by way of the gallery round the cemetery. Fountains, green trees, and rows of arcading maintained a cool freshness in keeping with the place.

At the further end of the long gallery the priest led the way into a large room divided in two by a grating covered with a brown curtain. In the first, and in some sort of public half of the apartment, where the confessor left the newcomer, a wooden bench ran round the wall, and two or three chairs, also of wood, were placed near the grating. The ceiling consisted of bare unornamented joists and cross-beams of ilex wood. As the two windows were both on the inner side of the grating, and the dark surface of the wood was a bad reflector, the light in the place was so dim that you could scarcely see the great black crucifix, the portrait of Saint Theresa, and a picture of the Madonna which adorned the grey parlour walls. Tumultuous as the General's feelings were, they took something of the melancholy of the place. He grew calm in that homely quiet. A sense of something vast as the tomb took possession of him beneath the chill unceiled roof. Here, as in the grave, was there not eternal silence, deep peace—the sense of the Infinite? And besides this there was the quiet and the fixed thought of the cloister—a thought which you felt like a subtle presence in the air, and in the dim dusk of the room; an all-pervasive thought nowhere definitely expressed, and looming the larger in the imagination; for in the cloister the great saying, "Peace in the Lord," enters the least religious soul as a living force.

The monk's life is scarcely comprehensible. A man seems confessed a weakling in a monastery; he was born to act, to live out a life of work; he is evading a man's destiny in his cell. But what man's strength, blended with pathetic weakness, is implied by a woman's choice of the convent life! A man may have any number of motives for burying himself in a monastery; for him it is the leap over the precipice. A woman has but one motive—she is a woman still; she betrothes herself to a Heavenly Bridegroom. Of the monk you may ask, "Why did you not fight your battle?" But if a woman immures herself in the cloister, is there not always a sublime battle fought first?

At length it seemed to the General that that still room, and the lonely convent in the sea, were full of thoughts of him. Love seldom attains to solemnity; yet surely a love still faithful in the breast of God was something solemn, something more than a man had a right to look for as things are in this nineteenth century? The infinite grandeur of the situation might well produce an effect upon the General's mind; he had precisely enough elevation of soul to forget politics, honours, Spain, and society in Paris, and to rise to the height of this lofty climax. And what in truth could be more tragic? How much must pass in the souls of these two lovers, brought together in a place of strangers, on a ledge of granite in the sea; yet held apart by an intangible, unsurmountable barrier! Try to imagine the man saying within himself, "Shall I triumph over God in her heart?" when a faint rustling sound made him quiver, and the curtain was drawn aside.

Between him and the light stood a woman. Her face was hidden by the veil that drooped from the folds upon her head; she was dressed according to the rule of the order in a gown of the colour become proverbial. Her bare feet were hidden; if the General could have seen them, he would have known how appallingly thin she had grown; and yet in spite of the thick folds of her coarse gown, a mere covering and no ornament, he could guess how tears, and prayer, and passion, and loneliness had wasted the woman before him.

An ice-cold hand, belonging, no doubt, to the Mother Superior, held back the curtain. The General gave the enforced witness of their interview a searching glance, and met the dark, inscrutable gaze of an aged recluse. The Mother might have been a century old, but the bright, youthful eyes belied the wrinkles that furrowed her pale face.

"Mme la Duchesse," he began, his voice shaken with emotion, "does your companion understand French?" The veiled figure bowed her head at the sound of his voice.

"There is no duchess here," she replied. "It is Sister Theresa whom you see before you. She whom you call my companion is my mother in God, my superior here on earth."

The words were so meekly spoken by the voice that sounded in other years amid harmonious surroundings of refined luxury, the voice of a queen of fashion in Paris. Such words from the lips that once spoke so lightly and flippantly struck the General dumb with amazement.

"The Holy Mother only speaks Latin and Spanish," she added.

"I understand neither. Dear Antoinette, make my excuses to her."

The light fell full upon the nun's figure; a thrill of deep emotion betrayed itself in a faint quiver of her veil as she heard her name softly spoken by the man who had been so hard in the past.

"My brother," she said, drawing her sleeve under her veil, perhaps to brush tears away, "I am Sister Theresa."

Then, turning to the Superior, she spoke in Spanish; the General knew enough of the language to understand what she said perfectly well; possibly he could have spoken it had he chosen to do so.

"Dear Mother, the gentleman presents his respects to you, and begs you to pardon him if he cannot pay them himself, but he knows neither of the languages which you speak——"

The aged nun bent her head slowly, with an expression of angelic sweetness, enhanced at the same time by the consciousness of her power and dignity.

"Do you know this gentleman?" she asked, with a keen glance.

"Yes, Mother."

"Go back to your cell, my daughter!" said the Mother imperiously.

The General slipped aside behind the curtain lest the dreadful tumult within him should appear in his face; even in the shadow it seemed to him that he could still see the Superior's piercing eyes. He was afraid of her; she held his little, frail, hardly-won happiness in her hands; and he, who had never quailed under a triple row of guns, now trembled before this nun. The Duchess went towards the door, but she turned back.

"Mother," she said, with dreadful calmness, "the Frenchman is one of my brothers."

"Then stay, my daughter," said the Superior, after a pause.

The piece of admirable Jesuitry told of such love and regret, that a man less strongly constituted might have broken down under the keen delight in the midst of a great and, for him, an entirely novel peril. Oh! how precious words, looks, and gestures became when love must baffle lynx eyes and tiger's claws! Sister Theresa came back.

"You see, my brother, what I have dared to do only to speak to you for a moment of your salvation and of the prayers that my soul puts up for your soul daily. I am committing mortal sin. I have told a lie. How many days of penance must expiate that lie! But I shall endure it for your sake. My brother, you do not know what happiness it is to love in heaven; to feel that you can confess love purified by religion, love transported into the highest heights of all, so that we are permitted to lose sight of all but the soul. If the doctrine and the spirit of the Saint to whom we owe this refuge had not raised me above earth's anguish, and caught me up and set me, far indeed beneath the Sphere wherein she dwells, yet truly above this world, I should not have seen you again. But now I can see you, and hear your voice, and remain calm— —"

The General broke in, "But, Antoinette, let me see you, you whom I love passionately, desperately, as you could have wished me to love you."

"Do not call me Antoinette, I implore you. Memories of the past hurt me. You must see no one here but Sister Theresa, a creature who trusts in the Divine mercy." She paused for a little, and then added, "You must control yourself, my brother. Our Mother would separate us without pity if there is any worldly passion in your face, or if you allow the tears to fall from your eyes."

The General bowed his head to regain self-control; when he looked up again he saw her face beyond the grating—the thin, white, but still impassioned face of the nun. All the magic charm of youth that once bloomed there, all the fair contrast of velvet whiteness and the colour of the Bengal rose, had given place to a burning glow, as of a porcelain jar with a faint light shining through it. The wonderful hair in which she took such pride had been shaven; there was a bandage round her forehead and about her face. An ascetic life had left dark traces about the eyes, which still sometimes shot out fevered glances; their ordinary calm expression was but a veil. In a few words, she was but the ghost of her former self.

"Ah! you that have come to be my life, you must come out of this tomb! You were mine; you had no right to give yourself, even to God. Did you not promise me to give up all at the least command from me? You may perhaps think me worthy of that promise now when you hear what I have done for you. I have sought you all through the world. You have been in my thoughts at every moment for five years; my life has been given to you. My friends, very powerful friends, as you know, have helped with all their might to search every convent in France, Italy, Spain, Sicily, and America. Love burned more brightly for every vain search. Again and again I made long journeys with a false hope; I have wasted my life and the heaviest throbbings of my heart in vain under many a dark convent wall. I am not speaking of a faithfulness that knows no bounds, for what is it?—nothing compared with the infinite longings of my love. If your remorse long ago was sincere, you ought not to hesitate to follow me today."

"You forget that I am not free."

"The Duke is dead," he answered quickly.

Sister Theresa flushed red.

"May heaven be open to him!" she cried with a quick rush of feeling. "He was generous to me.—But I did not mean such ties; it was one of my sins that I was ready to break them all without scruple—for you."

"Are you speaking of your vows?" the General asked, frowning. "I did not think that anything weighed heavier with your heart than love. But do not think twice of it, Antoinette; the Holy Father himself shall absolve you of your oath. I will surely go to Rome, I will entreat all the powers of earth; if God could come down from heaven, I would——"

"Do not blaspheme."

"So do not fear the anger of God. Ah! I would far rather hear that you would leave your prison for me; that this very night you would let yourself down into a boat at the foot of the cliffs. And we would go away to be happy somewhere at the world's end, I know not where. And with me at your side, you should come back to life and health under the wings of love."

"You must not talk like this," said Sister Theresa; "you do not know what you are to me now. I love you far better than I ever loved you before. Every day I pray for you; I see you with other eyes. Armand, if you but knew the happiness of giving yourself up, without shame, to a pure friendship which God watches over! You do not know what joy it is to me to pray for heaven's blessing on you. I never pray for myself: God will do with me according to His will; but, at the price of my soul, I wish I could be sure that you are happy here on earth, and that you will be happy hereafter throughout all ages. My eternal life is all that trouble has left me to offer up to you. I am old now with weeping; I am neither young nor fair; and in any case, you could not respect the nun who became a wife; no love, not even motherhood, could give me absolution.... What can you say to outweigh the uncounted thoughts that have gathered in my heart during the past five years, thoughts that have changed, and worn, and blighted it? I ought to have given a heart less sorrowful to God."

"What can I say? Dear Antoinette, I will say this, that I love you; that affection, love, a great love, the joy of living in another heart that is ours, utterly and wholly ours, is so rare a thing and so hard to find, that I doubted you, and put you to sharp proof; but now, today, I love you, Antoinette, with all my soul's strength.... If you will follow me into solitude, I will hear no voice but yours, I will see no other face."

"Hush, Armand! You are shortening the little time that we may be together here on earth."

"Antoinette, will you come with me?"

"I am never away from you. My life is in your heart, not through the selfish ties of earthly happiness, or vanity, or enjoyment; pale and withered as I am, I live here for you, in the breast of God. As God is just, you shall be happy——"

"Words, words all of it! Pale and withered? How if I want you? How if I cannot be happy without you? Do you still think of nothing but duty with your lover before you? Is he never to come first and above all things else in your heart? In time past you put social success, yourself, heaven knows what, before him; now it is God, it is the welfare of my soul! In Sister Theresa I find the Duchess over again, ignorant of the happiness of love, insensible as ever, beneath the semblance of sensibility. You do not love me; you have never loved me— —"

"Oh, my brother— —!"

"You do not wish to leave this tomb. You love my soul, do you say? Very well, through you it will be lost forever. I shall make away with myself— —"

"Mother!" Sister Theresa called aloud in Spanish, "I have lied to you; this man is my lover!"

The curtain fell at once. The General, in his stupor, scarcely heard the doors within as they clanged.

"Ah! she loves me still!" he cried, understanding all the sublimity of that cry of hers. "She loves me still. She must be carried off...."

The General left the island, returned to headquarters, pleaded ill-health, asked for leave of absence, and forthwith took his departure for France.

And now for the incidents which brought the two personages in this Scene into their present relation to each other.

The thing known in France as the Faubourg Saint-Germain is neither a Quarter, nor a sect, nor an institution, nor anything else that admits of a precise definition. There are great houses in the Place Royale, the Faubourg Saint-Honore, and the Chaussee d'Antin, in any one of which you may breathe the same atmosphere of Faubourg Saint-Germain. So, to begin with, the whole Faubourg is not within the Faubourg. There are men and women born far enough away from its influences who respond to them and take their place in the circle; and again there are others, born within its limits, who may yet be driven forth forever. For the last forty years the manners, and customs, and speech, in a word, the tradition of the Faubourg Saint-Germain, has been to Paris what the Court used to be in other times; it is what the Hotel Saint-Paul was to the fourteenth century; the Louvre to the fifteenth; the Palais, the Hotel Rambouillet, and the

Place Royale to the sixteenth; and lastly, as Versailles was to the seventeenth and the eighteenth.

Just as the ordinary workaday Paris will always centre about some point; so, through all periods of history, the Paris of the nobles and the upper classes converges towards some particular spot. It is a periodically recurrent phenomenon which presents ample matter for reflection to those who are fain to observe or describe the various social zones; and possibly an enquiry into the causes that bring about this centralization may do more than merely justify the probability of this episode; it may be of service to serious interests which some day will be more deeply rooted in the commonwealth, unless, indeed, experience is as meaningless for political parties as it is for youth.

In every age the great nobles, and the rich who always ape the great nobles, build their houses as far as possible from crowded streets. When the Duc d'Uzes built his splendid hotel in the Rue Montmartre in the reign of Louis XIV, and set the fountain at his gates—for which beneficent action, to say nothing of his other virtues, he was held in such veneration that the whole quarter turned out in a body to follow his funeral—when the Duke, I say, chose this site for his house, he did so because that part of Paris was almost deserted in those days. But when the fortifications were pulled down, and the market gardens beyond the line of the boulevards began to fill with houses, then the d'Uzes family left their fine mansion, and in our time it was occupied by a banker. Later still, the noblesse began to find themselves out of their element among shopkeepers, left the Place Royale and the centre of Paris for good, and crossed the river to breathe freely in the Faubourg Saint-Germain, where palaces were reared already about the great hotel built by Louis XIV for the Duc de Maine—the Benjamin among his legitimated offspring. And indeed, for people accustomed to a stately life, can there be more unseemly surroundings than the bustle, the mud, the street cries, the bad smells, and narrow thoroughfares of a populous quarter? The very habits of life in a mercantile or manufacturing district are completely at variance with the lives of nobles. The shopkeeper and artisan are just going to bed when the great world is thinking of dinner; and the noisy stir of life begins among the former when the latter have gone to rest. Their day's calculations never coincide; the one class represents the expenditure, the other the receipts. Consequently their manners and customs are diametrically opposed.

Nothing contemptuous is intended by this statement. An aristocracy is in a manner the intellect of the social system, as the middle classes and the proletariat may be said to be its organizing and working power. It naturally follows that these forces are differently situated; and of their antagonism there is bred a seeming antipathy produced by the performance of different functions, all of them, however, existing for one common end.

Such social dissonances are so inevitably the outcome of any charter of the constitution, that however much a Liberal may be disposed to complain of them, as of treason against those sublime ideas with which the ambitious plebeian is apt to cover his designs, he would none the less think it a preposterous notion that M. le Prince de Montmorency, for instance, should continue to live in the Rue Saint-Martin at the corner of the street which bears that nobleman's name; or that M. le Duc de Fitz-James, descendant of the royal house of Scotland, should have his hotel at the angle of the Rue Marie Stuart and the Rue Montorgueil. *Sint ut sunt, aut non sint*, the grand words of the Jesuit, might be taken as a motto by the great in all countries. These social differences are patent in all ages; the fact is always accepted by the people; its "reasons of state" are self-evident; it is at once cause and effect, a principle and a law. The common sense of the masses never deserts them until demagogues stir them up to gain ends of their own; that common sense is based on the verities of social order; and the social order is the same everywhere, in Moscow as in London, in Geneva as in Calcutta. Given a certain number of families of unequal fortune in any given space, you will see an aristocracy forming under your eyes; there will be the patricians, the upper classes, and yet other ranks below them. Equality may be a *right*, but no power on earth can convert it into *fact*. It would be a good thing for France if this idea could be popularized. The benefits of political harmony are obvious to the least intelligent classes. Harmony is, as it were, the poetry of order, and order is a matter of vital importance to the working population. And what is order, reduced to its simplest expression, but the agreement of things among themselves—unity, in short? Architecture, music, and poetry,

21

everything in France, and in France more than in any other country, is based upon this principle; it is written upon the very foundations of her clear accurate language, and a language must always be the most infallible index of national character. In the same way you may note that the French popular airs are those most calculated to strike the imagination, the best-modulated melodies are taken over by the people; clearness of thought, the intellectual simplicity of an idea attracts them; they like the incisive sayings that hold the greatest number of ideas. France is the one country in the world where a little phrase may bring about a great revolution. Whenever the masses have risen, it has been to bring men, affairs, and principles into agreement. No nation has a clearer conception of that idea of unity which should permeate the life of an aristocracy; possibly no other nation has so intelligent a comprehension of a political necessity; history will never find her behind the time. France has been led astray many a time, but she is deluded, woman-like, by generous ideas, by a glow of enthusiasm which at first outstrips sober reason.

So, to begin with, the most striking characteristic of the Faubourg is the splendour of its great mansions, its great gardens, and a surrounding quiet in keeping with princely revenues drawn from great estates. And what is this distance set between a class and a whole metropolis but visible and outward expression of the widely different attitude of mind which must inevitably keep them apart? The position of the head is well defined in every organism. If by any chance a nation allows its head to fall at its feet, it is pretty sure sooner or later to discover that this is a suicidal measure; and since nations have no desire to perish, they set to work at once to grow a new head. If they lack the strength for this, they perish as Rome perished, and Venice, and so many other states.

This distinction between the upper and lower spheres of social activity, emphasized by differences in their manner of living, necessarily implies that in the highest aristocracy there is real worth and some distinguishing merit. In any state, no matter what form of "government" is affected, so soon as the patrician class fails to maintain that complete superiority which is the condition of its existence, it ceases to be a force, and is pulled down at once by the populace. The people always wish to see money, power, and initiative in their leaders, hands, hearts, and heads; they must be the spokesmen, they must represent the intelligence and the glory of the nation. Nations, like women, love strength in those who rule them; they cannot give love without respect; they refuse utterly to obey those of whom they do not stand in awe. An aristocracy fallen into contempt is a *roi faineant*, a husband in petticoats; first it ceases to be itself, and then it ceases to be.

And in this way the isolation of the great, the sharply marked distinction in their manner of life, or in a word, the general custom of the patrician caste is at once the sign of a real power, and their destruction so soon as that power is lost. The Faubourg Saint-Germain failed to recognise the conditions of its being, while it would still have been easy to perpetuate its existence, and therefore was brought low for a time. The Faubourg should have looked the facts fairly in the face, as the English aristocracy did before them; they should have seen that every institution has its climacteric periods, when words lose their old meanings, and ideas reappear in a new guise, and the whole conditions of politics wear a changed aspect, while the underlying realities undergo no essential alteration.

These ideas demand further development which form an essential part of this episode; they are given here both as a succinct statement of the causes, and an explanation of the things which happen in the course of the story.

The stateliness of the castles and palaces where nobles dwell; the luxury of the details; the constantly maintained sumptuousness of the furniture; the "atmosphere" in which the fortunate owner of landed estates (a rich man before he was born) lives and moves easily and without friction; the habit of mind which never descends to calculate the petty workaday gains of existence; the leisure; the higher education attainable at a much earlier age; and lastly, the aristocratic tradition that makes of him a social force, for which his opponents, by dint of study and a strong will and tenacity of vocation, are scarcely a match-all these things should contribute to form a lofty spirit in a man, possessed of such privileges from his youth up; they should stamp his character with that high self-respect, of which the least consequence is a nobleness of heart in harmony with the noble name that he bears. And in some few

23

families all this is realised. There are noble characters here and there in the Faubourg, but they are marked exceptions to a general rule of egoism which has been the ruin of this world within a world. The privileges above enumerated are the birthright of the French noblesse, as of every patrician efflorescence ever formed on the surface of a nation; and will continue to be theirs so long as their existence is based upon real estate, or money; *domaine-sol* and *domaine-argent* alike, the only solid bases of an organized society; but such privileges are held upon the understanding that the patricians must continue to justify their existence. There is a sort of moral *fief* held on a tenure of service rendered to the sovereign, and here in France the people are undoubtedly the sovereigns nowadays. The times are changed, and so are the weapons. The knight-banneret of old wore a coat of chain armor and a hauberk; he could handle a lance well and display his pennon, and no more was required of him; today he is bound to give proof of his intelligence. A stout heart was enough in the days of old; in our days he is required to have a capacious brain-pan. Skill and knowledge and capital—these three points mark out a social triangle on which the scutcheon of power is blazoned; our modern aristocracy must take its stand on these.

A fine theorem is as good as a great name. The Rothschilds, the Fuggers of the nineteenth century, are princes *de facto*. A great artist is in reality an oligarch; he represents a whole century, and almost always he is a law to others. And the art of words, the high pressure machinery of the writer, the poet's genius, the merchant's steady endurance, the strong will of the statesman who concentrates a thousand dazzling qualities in himself, the general's sword—all these victories, in short, which a single individual will win, that he may tower above the rest of the world, the patrician class is now bound to win and keep exclusively. They must head the new forces as they once headed the material forces; how should they keep the position unless they are worthy of it? How, unless they are the soul and brain of a nation, shall they set its hands moving? How lead a people without the power of command? And what is the marshal's baton without the innate power of the captain in the man who wields it? The Faubourg Saint-Germain took to playing with batons, and fancied that all the power was in its hands. It inverted the terms of the proposition which called it into existence. And instead of flinging away the insignia which offended the people, and quietly grasping the power, it allowed the bourgeoisie to seize the authority, clung with fatal obstinacy to its shadow, and over and over again forgot the laws which a minority must observe if it would live. When an aristocracy is scarce a thousandth part of the body social, it is bound today, as of old, to multiply its points of action, so as to counterbalance the weight of the masses in a great crisis. And in our days those means of action must be living forces, and not historical memories.

In France, unluckily, the noblesse were still so puffed up with the notion of their vanished power, that it was difficult to contend against a kind of innate presumption in themselves. Perhaps this is a national defect. The Frenchman is less given than anyone else to undervalue himself; it comes natural to him to go from his degree to the one above it; and while it is a rare thing for him to pity the unfortunates over whose heads he rises, he always groans in spirit to see so many fortunate people above him. He is very far from heartless, but too often he prefers to listen to his intellect. The national instinct which brings the Frenchman to the front, the vanity that wastes his substance, is as much a dominant passion as thrift in the Dutch. For three centuries it swayed the noblesse, who, in this respect, were certainly pre-eminently French. The scion of the Faubourg Saint-Germain, beholding his material superiority, was fully persuaded of his intellectual superiority. And everything contributed to confirm him in his belief; for ever since the Faubourg Saint-Germain existed at all—which is to say, ever since Versailles ceased to be the royal residence—the Faubourg, with some few gaps in continuity, was always backed up by the central power, which in France seldom fails to support that side. Thence its downfall in 1830.

At that time the party of the Faubourg Saint-Germain was rather like an army without a base of operation. It had utterly failed to take advantage of the peace to plant itself in the heart of the nation. It sinned for want of learning its lesson, and through an utter incapability of regarding its interests as a whole. A future certainty was sacrificed to a doubtful present gain. This blunder in policy may perhaps be attributed to the following cause.

The class-isolation so strenuously kept up by the noblesse brought about fatal results during the last forty years; even caste-patriotism was extinguished by it, and rivalry fostered among themselves. When the French noblesse of other times were rich and powerful, the nobles (*gentilhommes*) could choose their chiefs and obey them in the hour of danger. As their power diminished, they grew less amenable to discipline; and as in the last days of the Byzantine Empire, everyone wished to be emperor. They mistook their uniform weakness for uniform strength.

Each family ruined by the Revolution and the abolition of the law of primogeniture thought only of itself, and not at all of the great family of the noblesse. It seemed to them that as each individual grew rich, the party as a whole would gain in strength. And herein lay their mistake. Money, likewise, is only the outward and visible sign of power. All these families were made up of persons who preserved a high tradition of courtesy, of true graciousness of life, of refined speech, with a family pride, and a squeamish sense of *noblesse oblige* which suited well with the kind of life they led; a life wholly filled with occupations which become contemptible so soon as they cease to be accessories and take the chief place in existence. There was a certain intrinsic merit in all these people, but the merit was on the surface, and none of them were worth their face-value.

Not a single one among those families had courage to ask itself the question, "Are we strong enough for the responsibility of power?" They were cast on the top, like the lawyers of 1830; and instead of taking the patron's place, like a great man, the Faubourg Saint-Germain showed itself greedy as an upstart. The most intelligent nation in the world perceived clearly that the restored nobles were organizing everything for their own particular benefit. From that day the noblesse was doomed. The Faubourg Saint-Germain tried to be an aristocracy when it could only be an oligarchy—two very different systems, as any man may see for himself if he gives an intelligent perusal to the list of the patronymics of the House of Peers.

The King's Government certainly meant well; but the maxim that the people must be made to *will* everything, even their own welfare, was pretty constantly forgotten, nor did they bear in mind that La France is a woman and capricious, and must be happy or chastised at her own good pleasure. If there had been many dukes like the Duc de Laval, whose modesty made him worthy of the name he bore, the elder branch would have been as securely seated on the throne as the House of Hanover at this day.

In 1814 the noblesse of France were called upon to assert their superiority over the most aristocratic bourgeoisie in the most feminine of all countries, to take the lead in the most highly educated epoch the world had yet seen. And this was even more notably the case in 1820. The Faubourg Saint-Germain might very easily have led and amused the middle classes in days when people's heads were turned with distinctions, and art and science were all the rage. But the narrow-minded leaders of a time of great intellectual progress all of them detested art and science. They had not even the wit to present religion in attractive colours, though they needed its support. While Lamartine, Lamennais, Montalembert, and other writers were putting new life and elevation into men's ideas of religion, and gilding it with poetry, these bunglers in the Government chose to make the harshness of their creed felt all over the country. Never was nation in a more tractable humour; La France, like a tired woman, was ready to agree to anything; never was mismanagement so clumsy; and La France, like a woman, would have forgiven wrongs more easily than bungling.

If the noblesse meant to reinstate themselves, the better to found a strong oligarchy, they should have honestly and diligently searched their Houses for men of the stamp that Napoleon used; they should have turned themselves inside out to see if peradventure there was a Constitutionalist Richelieu lurking in the entrails of the Faubourg; and if that genius was not forthcoming from among them, they should have set out to find him, even in the fireless garret where he might happen to be perishing of cold; they should have assimilated him, as the English House of Lords continually assimilates aristocrats made by chance; and finally ordered him to be ruthless, to lop away the old wood, and cut the tree down to the living shoots. But, in the first place, the great system of English Toryism was far too large for narrow minds; the importation required time, and in France a tardy success is no better than a fiasco. So far, moreover,

27

from adopting a policy of redemption, and looking for new forces where God puts them, these petty great folk took a dislike to any capacity that did not issue from their midst; and, lastly, instead of growing young again, the Faubourg Saint-Germain grew positively older.

Etiquette, not an institution of primary necessity, might have been maintained if it had appeared only on state occasions, but as it was, there was a daily wrangle over precedence; it ceased to be a matter of art or court ceremonial, it became a question of power. And if from the outset the Crown lacked an adviser equal to so great a crisis, the aristocracy was still more lacking in a sense of its wider interests, an instinct which might have supplied the deficiency. They stood nice about M. de Talleyrand's marriage, when M. de Talleyrand was the one man among them with the steel-encompassed brains that can forge a new political system and begin a new career of glory for a nation. The Faubourg scoffed at a minister if he was not gently born, and produced no one of gentle birth that was fit to be a minister. There were plenty of nobles fitted to serve their country by raising the dignity of justices of the peace, by improving the land, by opening out roads and canals, and taking an active and leading part as country gentlemen; but these had sold their estates to gamble on the Stock Exchange. Again the Faubourg might have absorbed the energetic men among the bourgeoisie, and opened their ranks to the ambition which was undermining authority; they preferred instead to fight, and to fight unarmed, for of all that they once possessed there was nothing left but tradition. For their misfortune there was just precisely enough of their former wealth left them as a class to keep up their bitter pride. They were content with their past. Not one of them seriously thought of bidding the son of the house take up arms from the pile of weapons which the nineteenth century flings down in the market-place. Young men, shut out from office, were dancing at Madame's balls, while they should have been doing the work done under the Republic and the Empire by young, conscientious, harmlessly employed energies. It was their place to carry out at Paris the programme which their seniors should have been following in the country. The heads of houses might have won back recognition of their titles by unremitting attention to local interests, by falling in with the spirit of the age, by recasting their order to suit the taste of the times.

But, pent up together in the Faubourg Saint-Germain, where the spirit of the ancient court and traditions of bygone feuds between the nobles and the Crown still lingered on, the aristocracy was not whole-hearted in its allegiance to the Tuileries, and so much the more easily defeated because it was concentrated in the Chamber of Peers, and badly organized even there. If the noblesse had woven themselves into a network over the country, they could have held their own; but cooped up in their Faubourg, with their backs against the Chateau, or spread at full length over the Budget, a single blow cut the thread of a fast-expiring life, and a petty, smug-faced lawyer came forward with the axe. In spite of M. Royer-Collard's admirable discourse, the hereditary peerage and law of entail fell before the lampoons of a man who made it a boast that he had adroitly argued some few heads out of the executioner's clutches, and now forsooth must clumsily proceed to the slaying of old institutions.

There are examples and lessons for the future in all this. For if there were not still a future before the French aristocracy, there would be no need to do more than find a suitable sarcophagus; it were something pitilessly cruel to burn the dead body of it with fire of Tophet. But though the surgeon's scalpel is ruthless, it sometimes gives back life to a dying man; and the Faubourg Saint-Germain may wax more powerful under persecution than in its day of triumph, if it but chooses to organize itself under a leader.

And now it is easy to give a summary of this semi-political survey. The wish to re-establish a large fortune was uppermost in everyone's mind; a lack of broad views, and a mass of small defects, a real need of religion as a political factor, combined with a thirst for pleasure which damaged the cause of religion and necessitated a good deal of hypocrisy; a certain attitude of protest on the part of loftier and clearer-sighted men who set their faces against Court jealousies; and the disaffection of the provincial families, who often came of purer descent than the nobles of the Court which alienated them from itself—all these things combined to bring about a most discordant state of things in the Faubourg Saint-Germain. It was neither compact in its organisation, nor consequent in its action; neither completely moral, nor frankly dissolute; it did not corrupt, nor was it corrupted; it would neither wholly abandon the disputed points which damaged its cause, nor yet adopt the policy that might have saved it. In short, however effete individuals might be, the party as a whole was none the less armed with all the great principles which lie at the roots of national existence. What was there in the Faubourg that it should perish in its strength?

It was very hard to please in the choice of candidates; the Faubourg had good taste, it was scornfully fastidious, yet there was nothing very glorious nor chivalrous truly about its fall.

In the Emigration of 1789 there were some traces of a loftier feeling; but in the Emigration of 1830 from Paris into the country there was nothing discernible but self-interest. A few famous men of letters, a few oratorical triumphs in the Chambers, M. de Talleyrand's attitude in the Congress, the taking of Algiers, and not a few names that found their way from the battlefield into the pages of history—all these things were so many examples set before the French noblesse to show that it was still open to them to take their part in the national existence, and to win recognition of their claims, if, indeed, they could condescend thus far. In every living organism the work of bringing the whole into harmony within itself is always going on. If a man is indolent, the indolence shows itself in everything that he does; and, in the same manner, the general spirit of a class is pretty plainly manifested in the face it turns on the world, and the soul informs the body.

The women of the Restoration displayed neither the proud disregard of public opinion shown by the court ladies of olden time in their wantonness, nor yet the simple grandeur of the tardy virtues by which they expiated their sins and shed so bright a glory about their names. There was nothing either very frivolous or very serious about the woman of the Restoration. She was hypocritical as a rule in her passion, and compounded, so to speak, with its pleasures. Some few families led the domestic life of the Duchesse d'Orleans, whose connubial couch was exhibited so absurdly to visitors at the Palais Royal. Two or three kept up the traditions of the Regency, filling cleverer women with something like disgust. The great lady of the new school exercised no influence at all over the manners of the time; and yet she might have done much. She might, at worst, have presented as dignified a spectacle as English-women of the same rank. But she hesitated feebly among old precedents, became a bigot by force of circumstances, and allowed nothing of herself to appear, not even her better qualities.

Not one among the Frenchwomen of that day had the ability to create a salon whither leaders of fashion might come to take lessons in taste and elegance. Their voices, which once laid down the law to literature, that living expression of a time, now counted absolutely for nought. Now when a literature lacks a general system, it fails to shape a body for itself, and dies out with its period.

When in a nation at any time there is a people apart thus constituted, the historian is pretty certain to find some representative figure, some central personage who embodies the qualities and the defects of the whole party to which he belongs; there is Coligny, for instance, among the Huguenots, the Coadjuteur in the time of the Fronde, the Marechal de Richelieu under Louis XV, Danton during the Terror. It is in the nature of things that the man should be identified with the company in which history finds him. How is it possible to lead a party without conforming to its ideas? or to shine in any epoch unless a man represents the ideas of his time? The wise and prudent head of a party is continually obliged to bow to the prejudices and follies of its rear; and this is the cause of actions for which he is afterwards criticised by this or that historian sitting at a safer distance from terrific popular explosions, coolly judging the passion and ferment without which the great struggles of the world could not be carried on at all. And if this is true of the Historical Comedy of the Centuries, it is equally true in a more restricted sphere in the detached scenes of the national drama known as the *Manners of the Age*.

At the beginning of that ephemeral life led by the Faubourg Saint-Germain under the Restoration, to which, if there is any truth in the above reflections, they failed to give stability, the most perfect type of the aristocratic caste in its weakness and strength, its greatness and littleness, might have been found for a brief space in a young married woman who belonged to it. This was a woman artificially educated, but in reality ignorant; a woman whose instincts and

31

feelings were lofty while the thought which should have controlled them was wanting. She squandered the wealth of her nature in obedience to social conventions; she was ready to brave society, yet she hesitated till her scruples degenerated into artifice. With more wilfulness than real force of character, impressionable rather than enthusiastic, gifted with more brain than heart; she was supremely a woman, supremely a coquette, and above all things a Parisienne, loving a brilliant life and gaiety, reflecting never, or too late; imprudent to the verge of poetry, and humble in the depths of her heart, in spite of her charming insolence. Like some straight-growing reed, she made a show of independence; yet, like the reed, she was ready to bend to a strong hand. She talked much of religion, and had it not at heart, though she was prepared to find in it a solution of her life. How explain a creature so complex? Capable of heroism, yet sinking unconsciously from heroic heights to utter a spiteful word; young and sweet-natured, not so much old at heart as aged by the maxims of those about her; versed in a selfish philosophy in which she was all unpractised, she had all the vices of a courtier, all the nobleness of developing womanhood. She trusted nothing and no one, yet there were times when she quitted her sceptical attitude for a submissive credulity.

How should any portrait be anything but incomplete of her, in whom the play of swiftly-changing colour made discord only to produce a poetic confusion? For in her there shone a divine brightness, a radiance of youth that blended all her bewildering characteristics in a certain completeness and unity informed by her charm. Nothing was feigned. The passion or semi-passion, the ineffectual high aspirations, the actual pettiness, the coolness of sentiment and warmth of impulse, were all spontaneous and unaffected, and as much the outcome of her own position as of the position of the aristocracy to which she belonged. She was wholly self-contained; she put herself proudly above the world and beneath the shelter of her name. There was something of the egoism of Medea in her life, as in the life of the aristocracy that lay a-dying, and would not so much as raise itself or stretch out a hand to any political physician; so well aware of its feebleness, or so conscious that it was already dust, that it refused to touch or be touched.

The Duchesse de Langeais (for that was her name) had been married for about four years when the Restoration was finally consummated, which is to say, in 1816. By that time the revolution of the Hundred Days had let in the light on the mind of Louis XVIII. In spite of his surroundings, he comprehended the situation and the age in which he was living; and it was only later, when this Louis XI, without the axe, lay stricken down by disease, that those about him got the upper hand. The Duchesse de Langeais, a Navarreins by birth, came of a ducal house which had made a point of never marrying below its rank since the reign of Louis XIV. Every daughter of the house must sooner or later take a *tabouret* at Court. So, Antoinette de Navarreins, at the age of eighteen, came out of the profound solitude in which her girlhood had been spent to marry the Duc de Langeais' eldest son. The two families at that time were living quite out of the world; but after the invasion of France, the return of the Bourbons seemed to every Royalist mind the only possible way of putting an end to the miseries of the war.

The Ducs de Navarreins and de Langeais had been faithful throughout to the exiled Princes, nobly resisting all the temptations of glory under the Empire. Under the circumstances they naturally followed out the old family policy; and Mlle Antoinette, a beautiful and portionless girl, was married to M. le Marquis de Langeais only a few months before the death of the Duke his father.

After the return of the Bourbons, the families resumed their rank, offices, and dignity at Court; once more they entered public life, from which hitherto they held aloof, and took their place high on the sunlit summits of the new political world. In that time of general baseness and sham political conversions, the public conscience was glad to recognise the unstained loyalty of the two houses, and a consistency in political and private life for which all parties involuntarily respected them. But, unfortunately, as so often happens in a time of transition, the most disinterested persons, the men whose loftiness of view and wise principles would have gained the confidence of the French nation and led them to believe in the generosity of a novel and spirited policy—these men, to repeat, were taken out of affairs, and public business was allowed to fall into the hands of others, who found it to their interest to push principles to their extreme consequences by way of proving their devotion.

The families of Langeais and Navarreins remained about the Court, condemned to perform the duties required by Court ceremonial amid the reproaches and sneers of the Liberal party. They were accused of gorging themselves with riches and honours, and all the while their family estates were no larger than before, and liberal allowances from the civil list were wholly expended in keeping up the state necessary for any European government, even if it be a Republic.

In 1818, M. le Duc de Langeais commanded a division of the army, and the Duchess held a post about one of the Princesses, in virtue of which she was free to live in Paris and apart from her husband without scandal. The Duke, moreover, besides his military duties, had a place at Court, to which he came during his term of waiting, leaving his major-general in command. The Duke and Duchess were leading lives entirely apart, the world none the wiser. Their marriage of convention shared the fate of nearly all family arrangements of the kind. Two more antipathetic dispositions could not well have been found; they were brought together; they jarred upon each other; there was soreness on either side; then they were divided once for all. Then they went their separate ways, with a due regard for appearances. The Duc de Langeais, by nature as methodical as the Chevalier de Folard himself, gave himself up methodically to his own tastes and amusements, and left his wife at liberty to do as she pleased so soon as he felt sure of her character. He recognised in her a spirit pre-eminently proud, a cold heart, a profound submissiveness to the usages of the world, and a youthful loyalty. Under the eyes of great relations, with the light of a prudish and bigoted Court turned full upon the Duchess, his honour was safe.

So the Duke calmly did as the *grands seigneurs* of the eighteenth century did before him, and left a young wife of two-and-twenty to her own devices. He had deeply offended that wife, and in her nature there was one appalling characteristic—she would never forgive an offence when woman's vanity and self-love, with all that was best in her nature perhaps, had been slighted, wounded in secret. Insult and injury in the face of the world a woman loves to forget; there is a way open to her of showing herself great; she is a woman in her forgiveness; but a secret offence women never pardon; for secret baseness, as for hidden virtues and hidden love, they have no kindness.

This was Mme la Duchesse de Langeais' real position, unknown to the world. She herself did not reflect upon it. It was the time of the rejoicings over the Duc de Berri's marriage. The Court and the Faubourg roused itself from its listlessness and reserve. This was the real beginning of that unheard-of splendour which the Government of the Restoration carried too far. At that time the Duchess, whether for reasons of her own, or from vanity, never appeared in public without a following of women equally distinguished by name and fortune. As queen of fashion she had her *dames d'atours*, her ladies, who modeled their manner and their wit on hers. They had been cleverly chosen. None of her satellites belonged to the inmost Court circle, nor to the highest level of the Faubourg Saint-Germain; but they had set their minds upon admission to those inner sanctuaries. Being as yet simple denominations, they wished to rise to the neighbourhood of the throne, and mingle with the seraphic powers in the high sphere known as *le petit chateau*. Thus surrounded, the Duchess's position was stronger and more commanding and secure. Her "ladies" defended her character and helped her to play her detestable part of a woman of fashion. She could laugh at men at her ease, play with fire, receive the homage on which the feminine nature is nourished, and remain mistress of herself.

At Paris, in the highest society of all, a woman is a woman still; she lives on incense, adulation, and honours. No beauty, however undoubted, no face, however fair, is anything without admiration. Flattery and a lover are proofs of power. And what is power without recognition? Nothing. If the prettiest of women were left alone in a corner of a drawing-room, she would droop. Put her in the very centre and summit of social grandeur, she will at once aspire to reign over all hearts—often because it is out of her power to be the happy queen of one. Dress and manner and coquetry are all meant to please one of the poorest creatures extant—the brainless coxcomb, whose handsome face is his sole merit; it was for such as these that women threw themselves away. The gilded wooden idols of the Restoration, for they were neither more nor less, had neither the antecedents of the *petits maitres* of the time of the Fronde, nor the rough sterling worth of Napoleon's heroes, not the wit and fine manners of their grandsires; but something of all three they meant to be without any trouble to themselves. Brave they were, like all young Frenchmen; ability they possessed, no doubt, if they had had a chance of proving it, but their places were filled up by the old worn-out men, who kept them in leading strings. It was a day of small things, a cold prosaic era. Perhaps it takes a long time for a Restoration to become a Monarchy.

For the past eighteen months the Duchesse de Langeais had been leading this empty life, filled with balls and subsequent visits, objectless triumphs, and the transient loves that spring up and die in an evening's space. All eyes were turned on her when she entered a room; she reaped her harvest of flatteries and some few words of warmer admiration, which she encouraged by a gesture or a glance, but never suffered to penetrate deeper than the skin. Her tone and bearing and everything else about her imposed her will upon others. Her life was a sort of fever of vanity and perpetual enjoyment, which turned her head. She was daring enough in conversation; she would listen to anything, corrupting the surface, as it were, of her heart. Yet when she returned home, she often blushed at the story that had made her laugh; at the scandalous tale that supplied the details, on the strength of which she analyzed the love that she had never known, and marked the subtle distinctions of modern passion, not with comment on the part of complacent hypocrites. For women know how to say everything among themselves, and more of them are ruined by each other than corrupted by men.

There came a moment when she discerned that not until a woman is loved will the world fully recognise her beauty and her wit. What does a husband prove? Simply that a girl or woman was endowed with wealth, or well brought up; that her mother managed cleverly that in some way she satisfied a man's ambitions. A lover constantly bears witness to her personal perfections. Then followed the discovery still in Mme de Langeais' early womanhood, that it was possible to be loved without committing herself, without permission, without vouchsafing any satisfaction beyond the most meagre dues.

There was more than one demure feminine hypocrite to instruct her in the art of playing such dangerous comedies.

So the Duchess had her court, and the number of her adorers and courtiers guaranteed her virtue. She was amiable and fascinating; she flirted till the ball or the evening's gaiety was at an end. Then the curtain dropped. She was cold, indifferent, self-contained again till the next day brought its renewed sensations, superficial as before. Two or three men were completely deceived, and fell in love in earnest. She laughed at them, she was utterly insensible. "I am loved!" she told herself. "He loves me!" The certainty sufficed her. It is enough for the miser to know that his every whim might be fulfilled if he chose; so it was with the Duchess, and perhaps she did not even go so far as to form a wish.

One evening she chanced to be at the house of an intimate friend Mme la Vicomtesse de Fontaine, one of the humble rivals who cordially detested her, and went with her everywhere. In a "friendship" of this sort both sides are on their guard, and never lay their armor aside; confidences are ingeniously indiscreet, and not unfrequently treacherous. Mme de Langeais had distributed her little patronizing, friendly, or freezing bows, with the air natural to a woman who knows the worth of her smiles, when her eyes fell upon a total stranger. Something in the man's large gravity of aspect startled her, and, with a feeling almost like dread, she turned to Mme de Maufrigneuse with, "Who is the newcomer, dear?"

"Someone that you have heard of, no doubt. The Marquis de Montriveau."

"Oh! is it he?"

She took up her eyeglass and submitted him to a very insolent scrutiny, as if he had been a picture meant to receive glances, not to return them.

"Do introduce him; he ought to be interesting."

"Nobody more tiresome and dull, dear. But he is the fashion."

M. Armand de Montriveau, at that moment all unwittingly the object of general curiosity, better deserved attention than any of the idols that Paris needs must set up to worship for a brief space, for the city is vexed by periodical fits of craving, a passion for *engouement* and sham enthusiasm, which must be satisfied. The Marquis was the only son of General de Montriveau, one of the *ci-devants* who served the Republic nobly, and fell by Joubert's side at Novi. Bonaparte had placed his son at the school at Chalons, with the orphans of other generals who fell on the battlefield, leaving their children under the protection of the Republic. Armand de Montriveau left school with his way to make, entered the artillery, and had only reached a major's rank at the time of the Fontainebleau disaster. In his section of the service the chances of advancement were not many. There are fewer officers, in the first place, among the gunners than in any other corps; and in the second place, the feeling in the artillery was decidedly Liberal, not to say Republican; and the Emperor, feeling little confidence in a body of highly educated men who were apt to think for themselves, gave promotion grudgingly in the service. In the artillery, accordingly, the general rule of the army did not apply; the commanding officers were not invariably the most remarkable men in their department, because there was less to be feared from mediocrities. The artillery was a separate corps in those days, and only came under Napoleon in action.

Besides these general causes, other reasons, inherent in Armand de Montriveau's character, were sufficient in themselves to account for his tardy promotion. He was alone in the world. He had been thrown at the age of twenty into the whirlwind of men directed by Napoleon; his interests were bounded by himself, any day he might lose his life; it became a habit of mind with him to live by his own self-respect and the consciousness that he had done his duty. Like all shy men, he was habitually silent; but his shyness sprang by no means from timidity; it was a kind of modesty in him; he found any demonstration of vanity intolerable. There was no sort of swagger about his fearlessness in action; nothing escaped his eyes; he could give sensible advice to his chums with unshaken coolness; he could go under fire, and duck upon occasion to avoid bullets. He was kindly; but his expression was haughty and stern, and his face gained him this character. In everything he was rigorous as arithmetic; he never permitted the slightest deviation from duty on any plausible pretext, nor blinked the consequences of a fact. He would lend himself to nothing of which he was ashamed; he never asked anything for himself; in short, Armand de Montriveau was one of many great men unknown to fame, and philosophical enough to despise it; living without attaching themselves to life, because they have not found their opportunity of developing to the full their power to do and feel.

People were afraid of Montriveau; they respected him, but he was not very popular. Men may indeed allow you to rise above them, but to decline to descend as low as they can do is the one unpardonable sin. In their feeling towards loftier natures, there is a trace of hate and fear. Too much honour with them implies censure of themselves, a thing forgiven neither to the living nor to the dead.

After the Emperor's farewells at Fontainebleau, Montriveau, noble though he was, was put on half-pay. Perhaps the heads of the War Office took fright at uncompromising uprightness worthy of antiquity, or perhaps it was known that he felt bound by his oath to the Imperial Eagle. During the Hundred Days he was made a Colonel of the Guard, and left on the field of Waterloo. His wounds kept him in Belgium he was not present at the disbanding of the Army of the Loire, but the King's government declined to recognise promotion made during the Hundred Days, and Armand de Montriveau left France.

An adventurous spirit, a loftiness of thought hitherto satisfied by the hazards of war, drove him on an exploring expedition through Upper Egypt; his sanity or impulse directed his enthusiasm to a project of great importance, he turned his attention to that unexplored Central Africa which occupies the learned of today. The scientific expedition was long and unfortunate. He had made a valuable collection of notes bearing on various geographical and commercial problems, of which solutions are still eagerly sought; and succeeded, after surmounting many obstacles, in reaching the heart of the continent, when he was betrayed into the hands of a hostile native tribe. Then, stripped of all that he had, for two years he led a wandering life in the desert, the slave of savages, threatened with death at every moment, and more cruelly treated than a dumb animal in the power of pitiless children. Physical strength, and a mind braced to endurance, enabled him to survive the horrors of that captivity; but his miraculous escape well-nigh exhausted his energies. When he reached the French colony at Senegal, a half-dead fugitive covered with rags, his memories of his former life were dim and shapeless. The great sacrifices made in his travels were all forgotten like his studies of African dialects, his discoveries, and observations. One story will give an idea of all that he passed through. Once for several days the children of the sheikh of the tribe amused themselves by putting him up for a mark and flinging horses' knuckle-bones at his head.

Montriveau came back to Paris in 1818 a ruined man. He had no interest, and wished for none. He would have died twenty times over sooner than ask a favour of anyone; he would not even press the recognition of his claims. Adversity and hardship had developed his energy even in trifles, while the habit of preserving his self-respect before that spiritual self which we call conscience led him to attach consequence to the most apparently trivial actions. His merits and adventures became known, however, through his acquaintances, among the principal men of science in Paris, and some few well-read military men. The incidents of his slavery and subsequent escape bore witness to a courage, intelligence, and coolness which won him celebrity without his knowledge, and that transient fame of which Paris salons are lavish, though the artist that fain would keep it must make untold efforts.

Montriveau's position suddenly changed towards the end of that year. He had been a poor man, he was now rich; or, externally at any rate, he had all the advantages of wealth. The King's government, trying to attach capable men to itself and to strengthen the army, made concessions about that time to Napoleon's old officers if their known loyalty and character offered guarantees of fidelity. M. de Montriveau's name once more appeared in the army list with the rank of colonel; he received his arrears of pay and passed into the Guards. All these favours, one after another, came to seek the Marquis de Montriveau; he had asked for nothing however small. Friends had taken the steps for him which he would have refused to take for himself.

After this, his habits were modified all at once; contrary to his custom, he went into society. He was well received, everywhere he met with great deference and respect. He seemed to have found some end in life; but everything passed within the man, there were no external signs; in society he was silent and cold, and wore a grave, reserved face. His social success was great, precisely because he stood out in such strong contrast to the conventional faces which line the walls of Paris salons. He was, indeed, something quite new there. Terse of speech, like a hermit or a savage, his shyness was thought to be haughtiness, and people were greatly taken with it. He was something strange and great. Women generally were so much the more smitten with this original person because he was not to be caught by their flatteries, however adroit, nor by the wiles with which they circumvent the strongest men and corrode the steel temper. Their Parisian's grimaces were lost upon M. de Montriveau; his nature only responded to the sonorous vibration of lofty thought and feeling. And he would very promptly have been dropped but for the romance that hung about his adventures and his life; but for the men who cried him up behind his back; but for a woman who looked for a triumph for her vanity, the woman who was to fill his thoughts.

For these reasons the Duchesse de Langeais' curiosity was no less lively than natural. Chance had so ordered it that her interest in the man before her had been aroused only the day before, when she heard the story of one of M. de Montriveau's adventures, a story calculated to make the strongest impression upon a woman's ever-changing fancy.

During M. de Montriveau's voyage of discovery to the sources of the Nile, he had had an argument with one of his guides, surely the most extraordinary debate in the annals of travel. The district that he wished to explore could only be reached on foot across a tract of desert. Only one of his guides knew the way; no traveller had penetrated before into that part of the country, where the undaunted officer hoped to find a solution of several scientific problems. In spite of the representations made to him by the guide and the older men of the place, he started upon the formidable journey. Summoning up courage, already highly strung by the prospect of dreadful difficulties, he set out in the morning.

The loose sand shifted under his feet at every step; and when, at the end of a long day's march, he lay down to sleep on the ground, he had never been so tired in his life. He knew, however, that he must be up and on his way before dawn next day, and his guide assured him that they should reach the end of their journey towards noon. That promise kept up his courage and gave him new strength. In spite of his sufferings, he continued his march, with some blasphemings against science; he was ashamed to complain to his guide, and kept his pain to himself. After marching for a third of the day, he felt his strength failing, his feet were bleeding, he asked if they should reach the place soon. "In an hour's time," said the guide. Armand braced himself for another hour's march, and they went on.

The hour slipped by; he could not so much as see against the sky the palm-trees and crests of hill that should tell of the end of the journey near at hand; the horizon line of sand was vast as the circle of the open sea.

He came to a stand, refused to go farther, and threatened the guide—he had deceived him, murdered him; tears of rage and weariness flowed over his fevered cheeks; he was bowed down with fatigue upon fatigue, his throat seemed to be glued by the desert thirst. The guide meanwhile stood motionless, listening to these complaints with an ironical expression, studying the while, with the apparent indifference of an Oriental, the scarcely perceptible indications in the lie of the sands, which looked almost black, like burnished gold.

"I have made a mistake," he remarked coolly. "I could not make out the track, it is so long since I came this way; we are surely on it now, but we must push on for two hours."

"The man is right," thought M. de Montriveau.

So he went on again, struggling to follow the pitiless native. It seemed as if he were bound to his guide by some thread like the invisible tie between the condemned man and the headsman. But the two hours went by, Montriveau had spent his last drops of energy, and the skyline was a blank, there were no palm-trees, no hills. He could neither cry out nor groan, he lay down on the sand to die, but his eyes would have frightened the boldest; something in his face seemed to say that he would not die alone. His guide, like a very fiend, gave him back a cool glance like a man that knows his power, left him to lie there, and kept at a safe distance out of reach of his desperate victim. At last M. Montriveau recovered strength enough for a last curse. The guide came nearer, silenced him with a steady look, and said, "Was it not your own will to go where I am taking you, in spite of us all? You say that I have lied to you. If I had not, you would not be even here. Do you want the truth? Here it is. *We have still another five hours' march before us, and we cannot go back.* Sound yourself; if you have not courage enough, here is my dagger."

Startled by this dreadful knowledge of pain and human strength, M. de Montriveau would not be behind a savage; he drew a fresh stock of courage from his pride as a European, rose to his feet, and followed his guide. The five hours were at an end, and still M. de Montriveau saw nothing, he turned his failing eyes upon his guide; but the Nubian hoisted him on his shoulders, and showed him a wide pool of water with greenness all about it, and a noble forest lighted up by the sunset. It lay only a hundred paces away; a vast ledge of granite hid the glorious landscape. It seemed to Armand that he had taken a new lease of life. His guide, that giant in courage and intelligence, finished his work of devotion by carrying him across the hot, slippery, scarcely discernible track on the granite. Behind him lay the hell of burning sand, before him the earthly paradise of the most beautiful oasis in the desert.

The Duchess, struck from the first by the appearance of this romantic figure, was even more impressed when she learned that this was that Marquis de Montriveau of whom she had dreamed during the night. She had been with him among the hot desert sands, he had been the companion of her nightmare wanderings; for such a woman was not this a delightful presage of a new interest in her life? And never was a man's exterior a better exponent of his character; never were curious glances so well justified. The principal characteristic of his great, square-hewn head was the thick, luxuriant black hair which framed his face, and gave him a strikingly close resemblance to General Kleber; and the likeness still held good in the vigorous forehead, in the outlines of his face, the quiet fearlessness of his eyes, and a kind of fiery vehemence expressed by strongly marked features. He was short, deep-chested, and muscular as a lion. There was something of the despot about him, and an indescribable suggestion of the security of strength in his gait, bearing, and slightest movements. He seemed to know that his will was irresistible, perhaps because he wished for nothing unjust. And yet, like all really strong men, he was mild of speech, simple in his manners, and kindly natured; although it seemed as if, in the stress of a great crisis, all these finer qualities must disappear, and the man would show himself implacable, unshaken in his resolve, terrific in action. There was a certain drawing in of the inner line of the lips which, to a close observer, indicated an ironical bent.

The Duchesse de Langeais, realising that a fleeting glory was to be won by such a conquest, made up her mind to gain a lover in Armand de Montriveau during the brief interval before the Duchesse de Maufrigneuse brought him to be introduced. She would prefer him above the others; she would attach him to herself, display all her powers of coquetry for him. It was a fancy, such a merest Duchess's whim as furnished a Lope or a Calderon with the plot of the *Dog in the Manger*. She would not suffer another woman to engross him; but she had not the remotest intention of being his.

Nature had given the Duchess every qualification for the part of coquette, and education had perfected her. Women envied her, and men fell in love with her, not without reason. Nothing that can inspire love, justify it, and give it lasting empire was wanting in her. Her style of beauty, her manner, her voice, her bearing, all combined to give her that instinctive coquetry which seems to be the consciousness of power. Her shape was graceful; perhaps there was a trace of self-consciousness in her changes of movement, the one affectation that could be laid to her charge; but everything about her was a part of her personality, from her least little gesture to the peculiar turn of her phrases, the demure glance of her eyes. Her great lady's grace, her most striking characteristic, had not destroyed the very French quick mobility of her person. There was an extraordinary fascination in her swift, incessant changes of attitude. She seemed as if she surely would be a most delicious mistress when her corset and the encumbering costume of her part were laid aside. All the rapture of love surely was latent in the freedom of her expressive glances, in her caressing tones, in the charm of her words.

She gave glimpses of the high-born courtesan within her, vainly protesting against the creeds of the duchess.

You might sit near her through an evening, she would be gay and melancholy in turn, and her gaiety, like her sadness, seemed spontaneous. She could be gracious, disdainful, insolent, or confiding at will. Her apparent good nature was real; she had no temptation to descend to malignity. But at each moment her mood changed; she was full of confidence or craft; her moving tenderness would give place to a heart-breaking hardness and insensibility. Yet how paint her as she was, without bringing together all the extremes of feminine nature? In a word, the Duchess was anything that she wished to be or to seem. Her face was slightly too long. There was a grace in it, and a certain thinness and fineness that recalled the portraits of the Middle Ages. Her skin was white, with a faint rose tint. Everything about her erred, as it were, by an excess of delicacy.

M. de Montriveau willingly consented to be introduced to the Duchesse de Langeais; and she, after the manner of persons whose sensitive taste leads them to avoid banalities, refrained from overwhelming him with questions and compliments. She received him with a gracious deference which could not fail to flatter a man of more than ordinary powers, for the fact that a man rises above the ordinary level implies that he possesses something of that tact which makes women quick to read feeling. If the Duchess showed any curiosity, it was by her glances; her compliments were conveyed in her manner; there was a winning grace displayed in her words, a subtle suggestion of a desire to please which she of all women knew the art of manifesting. Yet her whole conversation was but, in a manner, the body of the letter; the postscript with the principal thought in it was still to come. After half an hour spent in ordinary talk, in which the words gained all their value from her tone and smiles, M. de Montriveau was about to retire discreetly, when the Duchess stopped him with an expressive gesture.

"I do not know, monsieur, whether these few minutes during which I have had the pleasure of talking to you proved so sufficiently attractive, that I may venture to ask you to call upon me; I am afraid that it may be very selfish of me to wish to have you all to myself. If I should be so fortunate as to find that my house is agreeable to you, you will always find me at home in the evening until ten o'clock."

The invitation was given with such irresistible grace, that M. de Montriveau could not refuse to accept it. When he fell back again among the groups of men gathered at a distance from the women, his friends congratulated him, half laughingly, half in earnest, on the extraordinary reception vouchsafed him by the Duchesse de Langeais. The difficult and brilliant conquest had been made beyond a doubt, and the glory of it was reserved for the Artillery of the Guard. It is easy to imagine the jests, good and bad, when this topic had once been started; the world of Paris salons is so eager for amusement, and a joke lasts for such a short time, that everyone is eager to make the most of it while it is fresh.

All unconsciously, the General felt flattered by this nonsense. From his place where he had taken his stand, his eyes were drawn again and again to the Duchess by countless wavering reflections. He could not help admitting to himself that of all the women whose beauty had captivated his eyes, not one had seemed to be a more exquisite embodiment of faults and fair qualities blended in a completeness that might realise the dreams of earliest manhood. Is there a man in any rank of life that has not felt indefinable rapture in his secret soul over the woman singled out (if only in his dreams) to be his own; when she, in body, soul, and social aspects, satisfies his every requirement, a thrice perfect woman? And if this threefold perfection that flatters his pride is no argument for loving her, it is beyond cavil one of the great inducements to the sentiment. Love would soon be convalescent, as the eighteenth century moralist remarked, were it not for vanity. And it is certainly true that for everyone, man or woman, there is a wealth of pleasure in the superiority of the beloved. Is she set so high by birth that a contemptuous glance can never wound her? is she wealthy enough to surround herself with state which falls nothing short of royalty, of kings, of finance during their short reign of splendour? is she so ready-witted that a keen-edged jest never brings her into confusion? beautiful enough to rival any woman?—Is it such a small thing to know that your self-love will never suffer through her? A man makes these reflections in the twinkling of an eye. And how if, in the future opened out by early ripened passion, he catches glimpses of the changeful delight of her charm, the frank innocence of a maiden soul, the perils of love's voyage, the thousand folds of the veil of coquetry? Is not this enough to move the coldest man's heart?

This, therefore, was M. de Montriveau's position with regard to woman; his past life in some measure explaining the extraordinary fact. He had been thrown, when little more than a boy, into the hurricane of Napoleon's wars; his life had been spent on fields of battle. Of women he knew just so much as a traveller knows of a country when he travels across it in haste from one inn to another. The verdict which Voltaire passed upon his eighty years of life might, perhaps, have been applied by Montriveau to his own thirty-seven years of existence; had he not thirty-seven follies with which to reproach himself? At his age he was as much a novice in love as the lad that has just been furtively reading *Faublas*. Of women he had nothing to learn; of love he knew nothing; and thus, desires, quite unknown before, sprang from this virginity of feeling.

There are men here and there as much engrossed in the work demanded of them by poverty or ambition, art or science, as M. de Montriveau by war and a life of adventure—these know what it is to be in this unusual position if they very seldom confess to it. Every man in Paris is supposed to have been in love. No woman in Paris cares to take what other women have passed over. The dread of being taken for a fool is the source of the coxcomb's bragging so common in France; for in France to have the reputation of a fool is to be a foreigner in one's own country. Vehement desire seized on M. de Montriveau, desire that had gathered strength from the heat of the desert and the first stirrings of a heart unknown as yet in its suppressed turbulence.

A strong man, and violent as he was strong, he could keep mastery over himself; but as he talked of indifferent things, he retired within himself, and swore to possess this woman, for through that thought lay the only way to love for him. Desire became a solemn compact made with himself, an oath after the manner of the Arabs among whom he had lived; for among them a vow is a kind of contract made with Destiny a man's whole future is solemnly pledged to fulfil it, and everything even his own death, is regarded simply as a means to the one end.

A younger man would have said to himself, "I should very much like to have the Duchess for my mistress!" or, "If the Duchesse de Langeais cared for a man, he would be a very lucky rascal!" But the General said, "I will have Mme de Langeais for my mistress." And if a man takes such an idea into his head when his heart has never been touched before, and love begins to be a kind of religion with him, he little knows in what a hell he has set his foot.

Armand de Montriveau suddenly took flight and went home in the first hot fever-fit of the first love that he had known. When a man has kept all his boyish beliefs, illusions, frankness, and impetuosity into middle age, his first impulse is, as it were, to stretch out a hand to take the thing that he desires; a little later he realizes that there is a gulf set between them, and that it is all but impossible to cross it. A sort of childish impatience seizes him, he wants the thing the more, and trembles or cries. Wherefore, the next day, after the stormiest reflections that had yet perturbed his mind, Armand de Montriveau discovered that he was under the yoke of the senses, and his bondage made the heavier by his love.

The woman so cavalierly treated in his thoughts of yesterday had become a most sacred and dreadful power. She was to be his world, his life, from this time forth. The greatest joy, the keenest anguish, that he had yet known grew colorless before the bare recollection of the least sensation stirred in him by her. The swiftest revolutions in a man's outward life only touch his interests, while passion brings a complete revulsion of feeling. And so in those who live by feeling, rather than by self-interest, the doers rather than the reasoners, the sanguine rather than the lymphatic temperaments, love works a complete revolution. In a flash, with one single reflection, Armand de Montriveau wiped out his whole past life.

A score of times he asked himself, like a boy, "Shall I go, or shall I not?" and then at last he dressed, came to the Hotel de Langeais towards eight o'clock that evening, and was admitted. He was to see the woman—ah! not the woman—the idol that he had seen yesterday, among lights, a fresh innocent girl in gauze and silken lace and veiling. He burst in upon her to declare his love, as if it were a question of firing the first shot on a field of battle.

Poor novice! He found his ethereal sylphide shrouded in a brown cashmere dressing-gown ingeniously befrilled, lying languidly stretched out upon a sofa in a dimly lighted boudoir. Mme de Langeais did not so much as rise, nothing was visible of her but her face, her hair was loose but confined by a scarf. A hand indicated a seat, a hand that seemed white as marble to Montriveau by the flickering light of a single candle at the further side of the room, and a voice as soft as the light said:

"If it had been anyone else, M. le Marquis, a friend with whom I could dispense with ceremony, or a mere acquaintance in whom I felt but slight interest, I should have closed my door. I am exceedingly unwell."

"I will go," Armand said to himself.

"But I do not know how it is," she continued (and the simple warrior attributed the shining of her eyes to fever), "perhaps it was a presentiment of your kind visit (and no one can be more sensible of the prompt attention than I), but the vapors have left my head."

"Then may I stay?"

"Oh, I should be very sorry to allow you to go. I told myself this morning that it was impossible that I should have made the slightest impression on your mind, and that in all probability you took my request for one of the commonplaces of which Parisians are lavish on every occasion. And I forgave your ingratitude in advance. An explorer from the deserts is not supposed to know how exclusive we are in our friendships in the Faubourg."

The gracious, half-murmured words dropped one by one, as if they had been weighted with the gladness that apparently brought them to her lips. The Duchess meant to have the full benefit of her headache, and her speculation was fully successful. The General, poor man, was really distressed by the lady's simulated distress. Like Crillon listening to the story of the Crucifixion, he was ready to draw his sword against the vapors. How could a man dare to speak just then to this suffering woman of the love that she inspired?

Armand had already felt that it would be absurd to fire off a declaration of love point-blank at one so far above other women. With a single thought came understanding of the delicacies of feeling, of the soul's requirements. To love: what was that but to know how to plead, to beg for alms, to wait? And as for the love that he felt, must he not prove it? His tongue was mute, it was frozen by the conventions of the noble Faubourg, the majesty of a sick headache, the bashfulness of love. But no power on earth could veil his glances; the heat and the Infinite of the desert blazed in eyes calm as a panther's, beneath the lids that fell so seldom. The Duchess enjoyed the steady gaze that enveloped her in light and warmth.

"Mme la Duchesse," he answered, "I am afraid I express my gratitude for your goodness very badly. At this moment I have but one desire—I wish it were in my power to cure the pain."

"Permit me to throw this off, I feel too warm now," she said, gracefully tossing aside a cushion that covered her feet.

"Madame, in Asia your feet would be worth some ten thousand sequins.

"A traveler's compliment!" smiled she.

It pleased the sprightly lady to involve a rough soldier in a labyrinth of nonsense, commonplaces, and meaningless talk, in which he manoeuvred, in military language, as Prince Charles might have done at close quarters with Napoleon. She took a mischievous amusement in reconnoitring the extent of his infatuation by the number of foolish speeches extracted from a novice whom she led step by step into a hopeless maze, meaning to leave him there in confusion. She began by laughing at him, but nevertheless it pleased her to make him forget how time went.

The length of a first visit is frequently a compliment, but Armand was innocent of any such intent. The famous explorer spent an hour in chat on all sorts of subjects, said nothing that he meant to say, and was feeling that he was only an instrument on whom this woman played, when she rose, sat upright, drew the scarf from her hair, and wrapped it about her throat, leant her elbow on the cushions, did him the honour of a complete cure, and rang for lights. The most graceful movement succeeded to complete repose. She turned to M.

de Montriveau, from whom she had just extracted a confidence which seemed to interest her deeply, and said:

"You wish to make game of me by trying to make me believe that you have never loved. It is a man's great pretension with us. And we always believe it! Out of pure politeness. Do we not know what to expect from it for ourselves? Where is the man that has found but a single opportunity of losing his heart? But you love to deceive us, and we submit to be deceived, poor foolish creatures that we are; for your hypocrisy is, after all, a homage paid to the superiority of our sentiments, which are all purity."

The last words were spoken with a disdainful pride that made the novice in love feel like a worthless bale flung into the deep, while the Duchess was an angel soaring back to her particular heaven.

"Confound it!" thought Armand de Montriveau, "how am I to tell this wild thing that I love her?"

He had told her already a score of times; or rather, the Duchess had a score of times read his secret in his eyes; and the passion in this unmistakably great man promised her amusement, and an interest in her empty life. So she prepared with no little dexterity to raise a certain number of redoubts for him to carry by storm before he should gain an entrance into her heart. Montriveau should overleap one difficulty after another; he should be a plaything for her caprice, just as an insect teased by children is made to jump from one finger to another, and in spite of all its pains is kept in the same place by its mischievous tormentor. And yet it gave the Duchess inexpressible happiness to see that this strong man had told her the truth. Armand had never loved, as he had said. He was about to go, in a bad humour with himself, and still more out of humour with her; but it delighted her to see a sullenness that she could conjure away with a word, a glance, or a gesture.

"Will you come tomorrow evening?" she asked. "I am going to a ball, but I shall stay at home for you until ten o'clock."

Montriveau spent most of the next day in smoking an indeterminate quantity of cigars in his study window, and so got through the hours till he could dress and go to the Hotel de Langeais. To anyone who had known the magnificent worth of the man, it would have been grievous to see him grown so small, so distrustful of himself; the mind that might have shed light over undiscovered worlds shrunk to the proportions of a she-coxcomb's boudoir. Even he himself felt that he had fallen so low already in his happiness that to save his life he could not have told his love to one of his closest friends. Is there not always a trace of shame in the lover's bashfulness, and perhaps in woman a certain exultation over diminished masculine stature? Indeed, but for a host of motives of this kind, how explain why women are nearly always the first to betray the secret?—a secret of which, perhaps, they soon weary.

"Mme la Duchesse cannot see visitors, monsieur," said the man; "she is dressing, she begs you to wait for her here."

Armand walked up and down the drawing-room, studying her taste in the least details. He admired Mme de Langeais herself in the objects of her choosing; they revealed her life before he could grasp her personality and ideas. About an hour later the Duchess came noiselessly out of her chamber. Montriveau turned, saw her flit like a shadow across the room, and trembled. She came up to him, not with a bourgeoise's enquiry, "How do I look?" She was sure of herself; her steady eyes said plainly, "I am adorned to please you."

No one surely, save the old fairy godmother of some princess in disguise, could have wound a cloud of gauze about the dainty throat, so that the dazzling satin skin beneath should gleam through the gleaming folds. The Duchess was dazzling. The pale blue colour of her gown, repeated in the flowers in her hair, appeared by the richness of its hue to lend substance to a fragile form grown too wholly ethereal; for as she glided towards Armand, the loose ends of her scarf floated about her, putting that valiant warrior in mind of the bright damosel flies that hover now over water, now over the flowers with which they seem to mingle and blend.

"I have kept you waiting," she said, with the tone that a woman can always bring into her voice for the man whom she wishes to please.

"I would wait patiently through an eternity," said he, "if I were sure of finding a divinity so fair; but it is no compliment to speak of your beauty to you; nothing save worship could touch you. Suffer me only to kiss your scarf."

"Oh, fie!" she said, with a commanding gesture, "I esteem you enough to give you my hand."

She held it out for his kiss. A woman's hand, still moist from the scented bath, has a soft freshness, a velvet smoothness that sends a tingling thrill from the lips to the soul. And if a man is attracted to a woman, and his senses are as quick to feel pleasure as his heart is full of love, such a kiss, though chaste in appearance, may conjure up a terrific storm.

"Will you always give it me like this?" the General asked humbly when he had pressed that dangerous hand respectfully to his lips.

"Yes, but there we must stop," she said, smiling. She sat down, and seemed very slow over putting on her gloves, trying to slip the unstretched kid over all her fingers at once, while she watched M. de Montriveau; and he was lost in admiration of the Duchess and those repeated graceful movements of hers.

"Ah! you were punctual," she said; "that is right. I like punctuality. It is the courtesy of kings, His Majesty says; but to my thinking, from you men it is the most respectful flattery of all. Now, is it not? Just tell me."

Again she gave him a side glance to express her insidious friendship, for he was dumb with happiness sheer happiness through such nothings as these! Oh, the Duchess understood *son metier de femme*— the art and mystery of being a woman—most marvelously well; she knew, to admiration, how to raise a man in his own esteem as he humbled himself to her; how to reward every step of the descent to sentimental folly with hollow flatteries.

"You will never forget to come at nine o'clock."

"No; but are you going to a ball every night?"

"Do I know?" she answered, with a little childlike shrug of the shoulders; the gesture was meant to say that she was nothing if not capricious, and that a lover must take her as she was.—"Besides," she added, "what is that to you? You shall be my escort."

"That would be difficult tonight," he objected; "I am not properly dressed."

"It seems to me," she returned loftily, "that if anyone has a right to complain of your costume, it is I. Know, therefore, *monsieur le voyageur*, that if I accept a man's arm, he is forthwith above the laws of fashion, nobody would venture to criticise him. You do not know the world, I see; I like you the better for it."

And even as she spoke she swept him into the pettiness of that world by the attempt to initiate him into the vanities of a woman of fashion.

"If she chooses to do a foolish thing for me, I should be a simpleton to prevent her," said Armand to himself. "She has a liking for me beyond a doubt; and as for the world, she cannot despise it more than I do. So, now for the ball if she likes."

The Duchess probably thought that if the General came with her and appeared in a ballroom in boots and a black tie, nobody would hesitate to believe that he was violently in love with her. And the General was well pleased that the queen of fashion should think of compromising herself for him; hope gave him wit. He had gained confidence, he brought out his thoughts and views; he felt nothing of the restraint that weighed on his spirits yesterday. His talk was interesting and animated, and full of those first confidences so sweet to make and to receive.

Was Mme de Langeais really carried away by his talk, or had she devised this charming piece of coquetry? At any rate, she looked up mischievously as the clock struck twelve.

"Ah! you have made me too late for the ball!" she exclaimed, surprised and vexed that she had forgotten how time was going.

The next moment she approved the exchange of pleasures with a smile that made Armand's heart give a sudden leap.

"I certainly promised Mme de Beauseant," she added. "They are all expecting me."

"Very well—go."

"No—go on. I will stay. Your Eastern adventures fascinate me. Tell me the whole story of your life. I love to share in a brave man's hardships, and I feel them all, indeed I do!"

She was playing with her scarf, twisting it and pulling it to pieces, with jerky, impatient movements that seemed to tell of inward dissatisfaction and deep reflection.

"*We* are fit for nothing," she went on. "Ah! we are contemptible, selfish, frivolous creatures. We can bore ourselves with amusements, and that is all we can do. Not one of us that understands that she has a part to play in life. In old days in France, women were beneficent lights; they lived to comfort those that mourned, to encourage high virtues, to reward artists and stir new life with noble thoughts. If the world has grown so petty, ours is the fault. You make me loathe the ball and this world in which I live. No, I am not giving up much for you."

She had plucked her scarf to pieces, as a child plays with a flower, pulling away all the petals one by one; and now she crushed it into a ball, and flung it away. She could show her swan's neck.

She rang the bell. "I shall not go out tonight," she told the footman. Her long, blue eyes turned timidly to Armand; and by the look of misgiving in them, he knew that he was meant to take the order for a confession, for a first and great favour. There was a pause, filled with many thoughts, before she spoke with that tenderness which is often in women's voices, and not so often in their hearts. "You have had a hard life," she said.

"No," returned Armand. "Until today I did not know what happiness was."

"Then you know it now?" she asked, looking at him with a demure, keen glance.

"What is happiness for me henceforth but this—to see you, to hear you?... Until now I have only known privation; now I know that I can be unhappy — —"

"That will do, that will do," she said. "You must go; it is past midnight. Let us regard appearances. People must not talk about us. I do not know quite what I shall say; but the headache is a good-natured friend, and tells no tales."

"Is there to be a ball tomorrow night?"

"You would grow accustomed to the life, I think. Very well. Yes, we will go again tomorrow night."

There was not a happier man in the world than Armand when he went out from her. Every evening he came to Mme de Langeais' at the hour kept for him by a tacit understanding.

It would be tedious, and, for the many young men who carry a redundance of such sweet memories in their hearts, it were superfluous to follow the story step by step—the progress of a romance growing in those hours spent together, a romance controlled entirely by a woman's will. If sentiment went too fast, she would raise a quarrel over a word, or when words flagged behind her thoughts, she appealed to the feelings. Perhaps the only way of following such Penelope's progress is by marking its outward and visible signs.

As, for instance, within a few days of their first meeting, the assiduous General had won and kept the right to kiss his lady's insatiable hands. Wherever Mme de Langeais went, M. de Montriveau was certain to be seen, till people jokingly called him "Her Grace's orderly." And already he had made enemies; others were jealous, and envied him his position. Mme de Langeais had attained her end. The Marquis de Montriveau was among her numerous train of adorers, and a means of humiliating those who boasted of their progress in her good graces, for she publicly gave him preference over them all.

"Decidedly, M. de Montriveau is the man for whom the Duchess shows a preference," pronounced Mme de Serizy.

And who in Paris does not know what it means when a woman "shows a preference?" All went on therefore according to prescribed rule. The anecdotes which people were pleased to circulate concerning the General put that warrior in so formidable a light, that the more adroit quietly dropped their pretensions to the Duchess, and remained in her train merely to turn the position to account, and to use her name and personality to make better terms for themselves with certain stars of the second magnitude. And those lesser powers were delighted to take a lover away from Mme de Langeais. The Duchess was keen-sighted enough to see these desertions and treaties with the enemy; and her pride would not suffer her to be the dupe of them. As M. de Talleyrand, one of her great admirers, said, she knew how to take a second edition of revenge, laying the two-edged blade of a sarcasm between the pairs in these "morganatic" unions. Her mocking disdain contributed not a little to increase her reputation as an extremely clever woman and a person to be feared. Her character for virtue was consolidated while she amused herself with other people's secrets, and kept her own to herself. Yet, after two months of assiduities, she saw with a vague dread in the depths of her soul that M. de Montriveau understood nothing of the subtleties of flirtation after the manner of the Faubourg Saint-Germain; he was taking a Parisienne's coquetry in earnest.

"You will not tame *him*, dear Duchess," the old Vidame de Pamiers had said. "'Tis a first cousin to the eagle; he will carry you off to his eyrie if you do not take care."

Then Mme de Langeais felt afraid. The shrewd old noble's words sounded like a prophecy. The next day she tried to turn love to hate. She was harsh, exacting, irritable, unbearable; Montriveau disarmed her with angelic sweetness. She so little knew the great generosity of a large nature, that the kindly jests with which her first complaints were met went to her heart. She sought a quarrel, and found proofs of affection. She persisted.

"When a man idolizes you, how can he have vexed you?" asked Armand.

"You do not vex me," she answered, suddenly grown gentle and submissive. "But why do you wish to compromise me? For me you ought to be nothing but a *friend*. Do you not know it? I wish I could see that you had the instincts, the delicacy of real friendship, so that I might lose neither your respect nor the pleasure that your presence gives me."

"Nothing but your *friend!*" he cried out. The terrible word sent an electric shock through his brain. "On the faith of these happy hours that you grant me, I sleep and wake in your heart. And now today, for no reason, you are pleased to destroy all the secret hopes by which I live. You have required promises of such constancy in me, you have said so much of your horror of women made up of nothing

57

but caprice; and now do you wish me to understand that, like other women here in Paris, you have passions, and know nothing of love? If so, why did you ask my life of me? why did you accept it?"

"I was wrong, my friend. Oh, it is wrong of a woman to yield to such intoxication when she must not and cannot make any return."

"I understand. You have merely been coquetting with me, and — —"

"Coquetting?" she repeated. "I detest coquetry. A coquette Armand, makes promises to many, and gives herself to none; and a woman who keeps such promises is a libertine. This much I believed I had grasped of our code. But to be melancholy with humorists, gay with the frivolous, and politic with ambitious souls; to listen to a babbler with every appearance of admiration, to talk of war with a soldier, wax enthusiastic with philanthropists over the good of the nation, and to give to each one his little dole of flattery — it seems to me that this is as much a matter of necessity as dress, diamonds, and gloves, or flowers in one's hair. Such talk is the moral counterpart of the toilette. You take it up and lay it aside with the plumed head-dress. Do you call this coquetry? Why, I have never treated you as I treat everyone else. With you, my friend, I am sincere. Have I not always shared your views, and when you convinced me after a discussion, was I not always perfectly glad? In short, I love you, but only as a devout and pure woman may love. I have thought it over. I am a married woman, Armand. My way of life with M. de Langeais gives me liberty to bestow my heart; but law and custom leave me no right to dispose of my person. If a woman loses her honour, she is an outcast in any rank of life; and I have yet to meet with a single example of a man that realizes all that our sacrifices demand of him in such a case. Quite otherwise. Anyone can foresee the rupture between Mme de Beauseant and M. d'Ajuda (for he is going to marry Mlle de Rochefide, it seems), that affair made it clear to my mind that these very sacrifices on the woman's part are almost always the cause of the man's desertion. If you had loved me sincerely, you would have kept away for a time. — Now, I will lay aside all vanity for you; is not that something? What will not people say of a woman to whom no man attaches himself? Oh, she is heartless, brainless, soulless; and what is more, devoid of charm! Coquettes will not spare me. They will rob me of the very qualities

58

that mortify them. So long as my reputation is safe, what do I care if my rivals deny my merits? They certainly will not inherit them. Come, my friend; give up something for her who sacrifices so much for you. Do not come quite so often; I shall love you none the less."

"Ah!" said Armand, with the profound irony of a wounded heart in his words and tone. "Love, so the scribblers say, only feeds on illusions. Nothing could be truer, I see; I am expected to imagine that I am loved. But, there! —there are some thoughts like wounds, from which there is no recovery. My belief in you was one of the last left to me, and now I see that there is nothing left to believe in this earth."

She began to smile.

"Yes," Montriveau went on in an unsteady voice, "this Catholic faith to which you wish to convert me is a lie that men make for themselves; hope is a lie at the expense of the future; pride, a lie between us and our fellows; and pity, and prudence, and terror are cunning lies. And now my happiness is to be one more lying delusion; I am expected to delude myself, to be willing to give gold coin for silver to the end. If you can so easily dispense with my visits; if you can confess me neither as your friend nor your lover, you do not care for me! And I, poor fool that I am, tell myself this, and know it, and love you!"

"But, dear me, poor Armand, you are flying into a passion!"

"I flying into a passion?"

"Yes. You think that the whole question is opened because I ask you to be careful."

In her heart of hearts she was delighted with the anger that leapt out in her lover's eyes. Even as she tortured him, she was criticising him, watching every slightest change that passed over his face. If the General had been so unluckily inspired as to show himself generous without discussion (as happens occasionally with some artless souls), he would have been a banished man forever, accused and convicted of not knowing how to love. Most women are not displeased to have their code of right and wrong broken through. Do they not flatter themselves that they never yield except to force? But

Armand was not learned enough in this kind of lore to see the snare ingeniously spread for him by the Duchess. So much of the child was there in the strong man in love.

"If all you want is to preserve appearances," he began in his simplicity, "I am willing to— —"

"Simply to preserve appearances!" the lady broke in; "why, what idea can you have of me? Have I given you the slightest reason to suppose that I can be yours?"

"Why, what else are we talking about?" demanded Montriveau.

"Monsieur, you frighten me!... No, pardon me. Thank you," she added, coldly; "thank you, Armand. You have given me timely warning of imprudence; committed quite unconsciously, believe it, my friend. You know how to endure, you say. I also know how to endure. We will not see each other for a time; and then, when both of us have contrived to recover calmness to some extent, we will think about arrangements for a happiness sanctioned by the world. I am young, Armand; a man with no delicacy might tempt a woman of four-and-twenty to do many foolish, wild things for his sake. But *you*! You will be my friend, promise me that you will?"

"The woman of four-and-twenty," returned he, "knows what she is about."

He sat down on the sofa in the boudoir, and leant his head on his hands.

"Do you love me, madame?" he asked at length, raising his head, and turning a face full of resolution upon her. "Say it straight out; Yes or No!"

His direct question dismayed the Duchess more than a threat of suicide could have done; indeed, the woman of the nineteenth century is not to be frightened by that stale stratagem, the sword has ceased to be part of the masculine costume. But in the effect of eyelids and lashes, in the contraction of the gaze, in the twitching of the lips, is there not some influence that communicates the terror which they express with such vivid magnetic power?

"Ah, if I were free, if— —"

"Oh! is it only your husband that stands in the way?" the General exclaimed joyfully, as he strode to and fro in the boudoir. "Dear Antoinette, I wield a more absolute power than the Autocrat of all the Russias. I have a compact with Fate; I can advance or retard destiny, so far as men are concerned, at my fancy, as you alter the hands of a watch. If you can direct the course of fate in our political machinery, it simply means (does it not?) that you understand the ins and outs of it. You shall be free before very long, and then you must remember your promise."

"Armand!" she cried. "What do you mean? Great heavens! Can you imagine that I am to be the prize of a crime? Do you want to kill me? Why! you cannot have any religion in you! For my own part, I fear God. M. de Langeais may have given me reason to hate him, but I wish him no manner of harm."

M. de Montriveau beat a tattoo on the marble chimney-piece, and only looked composedly at the lady.

"Dear," continued she, "respect him. He does not love me, he is not kind to me, but I have duties to fulfil with regard to him. What would I not do to avert the calamities with which you threaten him?—Listen," she continued after a pause, "I will not say another word about separation; you shall come here as in the past, and I will still give you my forehead to kiss. If I refused once or twice, it was pure coquetry, indeed it was. But let us understand each other," she added as he came closer. "You will permit me to add to the number of my satellites; to receive even more visitors in the morning than heretofore; I mean to be twice as frivolous; I mean to use you to all appearance very badly; to feign a rupture; you must come not quite so often, and then, afterwards——"

While she spoke, she had allowed him to put an arm about her waist, Montriveau was holding her tightly to him, and she seemed to feel the exceeding pleasure that women usually feel in that close contact, an earnest of the bliss of a closer union. And then, doubtless she meant to elicit some confidence, for she raised herself on tiptoe, and laid her forehead against Armand's burning lips.

"And then," Montriveau finished her sentence for her, "you shall not speak to me of your husband. You ought not to think of him again."

61

Mme de Langeais was silent awhile.

"At least," she said, after a significant pause, "at least you will do all that I wish without grumbling, you will not be naughty; tell me so, my friend? You wanted to frighten me, did you not? Come, now, confess it?... You are too good ever to think of crimes. But is it possible that you can have secrets that I do not know? How can you control Fate?"

"Now, when you confirm the gift of the heart that you have already given me, I am far too happy to know exactly how to answer you. I can trust you, Antoinette; I shall have no suspicion, no unfounded jealousy of you. But if accident should set you free, we shall be one —
—"

"Accident, Armand?" (With that little dainty turn of the head that seems to say so many things, a gesture that such women as the Duchess can use on light occasions, as a great singer can act with her voice.) "Pure accident," she repeated. "Mind that. If anything should happen to M. de Langeais by your fault, I should never be yours."

And so they parted, mutually content. The Duchess had made a pact that left her free to prove to the world by words and deeds that M. de Montriveau was no lover of hers. And as for him, the wily Duchess vowed to tire him out. He should have nothing of her beyond the little concessions snatched in the course of contests that she could stop at her pleasure. She had so pretty an art of revoking the grant of yesterday, she was so much in earnest in her purpose to remain technically virtuous, that she felt that there was not the slightest danger for her in preliminaries fraught with peril for a woman less sure of her self-command. After all, the Duchess was practically separated from her husband; a marriage long since annulled was no great sacrifice to make to her love.

Montriveau on his side was quite happy to win the vaguest promise, glad once for all to sweep aside, with all scruples of conjugal fidelity, her stock of excuses for refusing herself to his love. He had gained ground a little, and congratulated himself. And so for a time he took unfair advantage of the rights so hardly won. More a boy than he had ever been in his life, he gave himself up to all the childishness that makes first love the flower of life. He was a child again as he poured out all his soul, all the thwarted forces that passion had given him, upon her hands, upon the dazzling forehead that looked so pure to his eyes; upon her fair hair; on the tufted curls where his lips were pressed. And the Duchess, on whom his love was poured like a flood, was vanquished by the magnetic influence of her lover's warmth; she hesitated to begin the quarrel that must part them forever. She was more a woman than she thought, this slight creature, in her effort to reconcile the demands of religion with the ever-new sensations of vanity, the semblance of pleasure which turns a Parisienne's head. Every Sunday she went to Mass; she never missed a service; then, when evening came, she was steeped in the intoxicating bliss of repressed desire. Armand and Mme de Langeais, like Hindoo fakirs, found the reward of their continence in the temptations to which it gave rise. Possibly, the Duchess had ended by resolving love into fraternal caresses, harmless enough, as it might have seemed to the rest of the world, while they borrowed extremes of degradation from the license of her thoughts. How else explain the incomprehensible mystery of her continual fluctuations? Every morning she proposed to herself to shut her door on the Marquis de Montriveau; every evening, at the appointed hour, she fell under the charm of his presence. There was a languid defence; then she grew less unkind. Her words were sweet and soothing. They were lovers—lovers only could have been thus. For him the Duchess would display her most sparkling wit, her most captivating wiles; and when at last she had wrought upon his senses and his soul, she might submit herself passively to his fierce caresses, but she had her *nec plus ultra* of passion; and when once it was reached, she grew angry if he lost the mastery of himself and made as though he would pass beyond. No woman on earth can brave the consequences of refusal without some motive; nothing is more natural than to yield to love; wherefore Mme de Langeais promptly raised a second line of fortification, a stronghold less easy to carry than the first. She evoked the terrors of religion. Never did Father of the Church, however eloquent, plead the cause of God better than the Duchess. Never was the wrath of the Most High better justified than by her voice. She used no preacher's commonplaces, no rhetorical amplifications. No. She had a "pulpit-tremor" of her own. To Armand's most passionate entreaty, she replied with a tearful gaze, and a gesture in which a terrible plenitude of emotion found expression. She stopped his mouth with an appeal for mercy. She would not hear another word; if she did, she must succumb; and better death than criminal happiness.

"Is it nothing to disobey God?" she asked him, recovering a voice grown faint in the crises of inward struggles, through which the fair actress appeared to find it hard to preserve her self-control. "I would sacrifice society, I would give up the whole world for you, gladly; but it is very selfish of you to ask my whole after-life of me for a moment of pleasure. Come, now! are you not happy?" she added, holding out her hand; and certainly in her careless toilette the sight of her afforded consolations to her lover, who made the most of them.

Sometimes from policy, to keep her hold on a man whose ardent passion gave her emotions unknown before, sometimes in weakness, she suffered him to snatch a swift kiss; and immediately, in feigned terror, she flushed red and exiled Armand from the sofa so soon as the sofa became dangerous ground.

"Your joys are sins for me to expiate, Armand; they are paid for by penitence and remorse," she cried.

And Montriveau, now at two chairs' distance from that aristocratic petticoat, betook himself to blasphemy and railed against Providence. The Duchess grew angry at such times.

"My friend," she said drily, "I do not understand why you decline to believe in God, for it is impossible to believe in man. Hush, do not talk like that. You have too great a nature to take up their Liberal nonsense with its pretension to abolish God."

Theological and political disputes acted like a cold douche on Montriveau; he calmed down; he could not return to love when the Duchess stirred up his wrath by suddenly setting him down a thousand miles away from the boudoir, discussing theories of absolute monarchy, which she defended to admiration. Few women venture to be democrats; the attitude of democratic champion is scarcely compatible with tyrannous feminine sway. But often, on the other hand, the General shook out his mane, dropped politics with a leonine growling and lashing of the flanks, and sprang upon his prey; he was no longer capable of carrying a heart and brain at such variance for very far; he came back, terrible with love, to his mistress. And she, if she felt the prick of fancy stimulated to a dangerous point, knew that it was time to leave her boudoir; she came out of the atmosphere surcharged with desires that she drew in with her breath, sat down to the piano, and sang the most exquisite songs of modern music, and so baffled the physical attraction which at times showed her no mercy, though she was strong enough to fight it down.

At such times she was something sublime in Armand's eyes; she was not acting, she was genuine; the unhappy lover was convinced that she loved him. Her egoistic resistance deluded him into a belief that she was a pure and sainted woman; he resigned himself; he talked of Platonic love, did this artillery officer!

When Mme de Langeais had played with religion sufficiently to suit her own purposes, she played with it again for Armand's benefit. She wanted to bring him back to a Christian frame of mind; she brought out her edition of *Le Genie du Christianisme*, adapted for the use of military men. Montriveau chafed; his yoke was heavy. Oh! at that, possessed by the spirit of contradiction, she dinned religion into his ears, to see whether God might not rid her of this suitor, for the man's persistence was beginning to frighten her. And in any case she was glad to prolong any quarrel, if it bade fair to keep the dispute on moral grounds for an indefinite period; the material struggle which followed it was more dangerous.

But if the time of her opposition on the ground of the marriage law might be said to be the *epoque civile* of this sentimental warfare, the ensuing phase which might be taken to constitute the *epoque religieuse* had also its crisis and consequent decline of severity.

Armand happening to come in very early one evening, found M. l'Abbe Gondrand, the Duchess's spiritual director, established in an armchair by the fireside, looking as a spiritual director might be expected to look while digesting his dinner and the charming sins of his penitent. In the ecclesiastic's bearing there was a stateliness befitting a dignitary of the Church; and the episcopal violet hue already appeared in his dress. At sight of his fresh, well-preserved complexion, smooth forehead, and ascetic's mouth, Montriveau's countenance grew uncommonly dark; he said not a word under the malicious scrutiny of the other's gaze, and greeted neither the lady nor the priest. The lover apart, Montriveau was not wanting in tact; so a few glances exchanged with the bishop-designate told him that here was the real forger of the Duchess's armory of scruples.

That an ambitious abbe should control the happiness of a man of Montriveau's temper, and by underhand ways! The thought burst in a furious tide over his face, clenched his fists, and set him chafing and pacing to and fro; but when he came back to his place intending to make a scene, a single look from the Duchess was enough. He was quiet.

Any other woman would have been put out by her lover's gloomy silence; it was quite otherwise with Mme de Langeais. She continued her conversation with M. de Gondrand on the necessity of re-establishing the Church in its ancient splendour. And she talked brilliantly.

The Church, she maintained, ought to be a temporal as well as a spiritual power, stating her case better than the Abbe had done, and regretting that the Chamber of Peers, unlike the English House of Lords, had no bench of bishops. Nevertheless, the Abbe rose, yielded his place to the General, and took his leave, knowing that in Lent he could play a return game. As for the Duchess, Montriveau's behaviour had excited her curiosity to such a pitch that she scarcely rose to return her director's low bow.

"What is the matter with you, my friend?"

"Why, I cannot stomach that Abbe of yours."

"Why did you not take a book?" she asked, careless whether the Abbe, then closing the door, heard her or no.

The General paused, for the gesture which accompanied the Duchess's speech further increased the exceeding insolence of her words.

"My dear Antoinette, thank you for giving love precedence of the Church; but, for pity's sake, allow me to ask one question."

"Oh! you are questioning me! I am quite willing. You are my friend, are you not? I certainly can open the bottom of my heart to you; you will see only one image there."

"Do you talk about our love to that man?"

"He is my confessor."

"Does he know that I love you?"

"M. de Montriveau, you cannot claim, I think, to penetrate the secrets of the confessional?"

"Does that man know all about our quarrels and my love for you?"

"That man, monsieur; say God!"

"God again! *I* ought to be alone in your heart. But leave God alone where He is, for the love of God and me. Madame, you *shall not* go to confession again, or — —"

"Or?" she repeated sweetly.

"Or I will never come back here."

"Then go, Armand. Good-bye, good-bye forever."

She rose and went to her boudoir without so much as a glance at Armand, as he stood with his hand on the back of a chair. How long he stood there motionless he himself never knew. The soul within has the mysterious power of expanding as of contracting space.

He opened the door of the boudoir. It was dark within. A faint voice was raised to say sharply:

"I did not ring. What made you come in without orders? Go away, Suzette."

"Then you are ill," exclaimed Montriveau.

"Stand up, monsieur, and go out of the room for a minute at any rate," she said, ringing the bell.

"Mme la Duchesse rang for lights?" said the footman, coming in with the candles. When the lovers were alone together, Mme de Langeais still lay on her couch; she was just as silent and motionless as if Montriveau had not been there.

"Dear, I was wrong," he began, a note of pain and a sublime kindness in his voice. "Indeed, I would not have you without religion——"

"It is fortunate that you can recognise the necessity of a conscience," she said in a hard voice, without looking at him. "I thank you in God's name."

The General was broken down by her harshness; this woman seemed as if she could be at will a sister or a stranger to him. He made one despairing stride towards the door. He would leave her forever without another word. He was wretched; and the Duchess was laughing within herself over mental anguish far more cruel than the old judicial torture. But as for going away, it was not in his power to do it. In any sort of crisis, a woman is, as it were, bursting with a certain quantity of things to say; so long as she has not delivered herself of them, she experiences the sensation which we are apt to feel at the sight of something incomplete. Mme de Langeais had not said all that was in her mind. She took up her parable and said:

"We have not the same convictions, General, I am pained to think. It would be dreadful if a woman could not believe in a religion which permits us to love beyond the grave. I set Christian sentiments aside; you cannot understand them. Let me simply speak to you of expediency. Would you forbid a woman at court the table of the Lord when it is customary to take the sacrament at Easter? People must certainly do something for their party. The Liberals, whatever they may wish to do, will never destroy the religious instinct. Religion will always be a political necessity. Would you undertake to govern a nation of logic-choppers? Napoleon was afraid to try; he persecuted ideologists. If you want to keep people from reasoning, you must give them something to feel. So let us accept the Roman Catholic Church with all its consequences. And if we would have France go to mass, ought we not to begin by going ourselves? Religion, you see, Armand, is a bond uniting all the conservative principles which enable the rich to live in tranquillity. Religion and the rights of property are intimately connected. It is certainly a finer thing to lead a nation by ideas of morality than by fear of the scaffold, as in the time of the Terror—the one method by which your

68

odious Revolution could enforce obedience. The priest and the king—that means you, and me, and the Princess my neighbour; and, in a word, the interests of all honest people personified. There, my friend, just be so good as to belong to your party, you that might be its Scylla if you had the slightest ambition that way. I know nothing about politics myself; I argue from my own feelings; but still I know enough to guess that society would be overturned if people were always calling its foundations in question——"

"If that is how your Court and your Government think, I am sorry for you," broke in Montriveau. "The Restoration, madam, ought to say, like Catherine de Medici, when she heard that the battle of Dreux was lost, 'Very well; now we will go to the meeting-house.' Now 1815 was your battle of Dreux. Like the royal power of those days, you won in fact, while you lost in right. Political Protestantism has gained an ascendancy over people's minds. If you have no mind to issue your Edict of Nantes; or if, when it is issued, you publish a Revocation; if you should one day be accused and convicted of repudiating the Charter, which is simply a pledge given to maintain the interests established under the Republic, then the Revolution will rise again, terrible in her strength, and strike but a single blow. It will not be the Revolution that will go into exile; she is the very soil of France. Men die, but people's interests do not die. ... Eh, great Heavens! what are France and the crown and rightful sovereigns, and the whole world besides, to us? Idle words compared with my happiness. Let them reign or be hurled from the throne, little do I care. Where am I now?"

"In the Duchesse de Langeais' boudoir, my friend."

"No, no. No more of the Duchess, no more of Langeais; I am with my dear Antoinette."

"Will you do me the pleasure to stay where you are," she said, laughing and pushing him back, gently however.

"So you have never loved me," he retorted, and anger flashed in lightning from his eyes.

"No, dear"; but the "No" was equivalent to "Yes."

"I am a great ass," he said, kissing her hands. The terrible queen was a woman once more. — "Antoinette," he went on, laying his head on her feet, "you are too chastely tender to speak of our happiness to anyone in this world."

"Oh!" she cried, rising to her feet with a swift, graceful spring, "you are a great simpleton." And without another word she fled into the drawing-room.

"What is it now?" wondered the General, little knowing that the touch of his burning forehead had sent a swift electric thrill through her from foot to head.

In hot wrath he followed her to the drawing-room, only to hear divinely sweet chords. The Duchess was at the piano. If the man of science or the poet can at once enjoy and comprehend, bringing his intelligence to bear upon his enjoyment without loss of delight, he is conscious that the alphabet and phraseology of music are but cunning instruments for the composer, like the wood and copper wire under the hands of the executant. For the poet and the man of science there is a music existing apart, underlying the double expression of this language of the spirit and senses. *Andiamo mio ben* can draw tears of joy or pitying laughter at the will of the singer; and not unfrequently one here and there in the world, some girl unable to live and bear the heavy burden of an unguessed pain, some man whose soul vibrates with the throb of passion, may take up a musical theme, and lo! heaven is opened for them, or they find a language for themselves in some sublime melody, some song lost to the world.

The General was listening now to such a song; a mysterious music unknown to all other ears, as the solitary plaint of some mateless bird dying alone in a virgin forest.

"Great Heavens! what are you playing there?" he asked in an unsteady voice.

"The prelude of a ballad, called, I believe, *Fleuve du Tage*."

"I did not know that there was such music in a piano," he returned.

"Ah!" she said, and for the first time she looked at him as a woman looks at the man she loves, "nor do you know, my friend, that I love you, and that you cause me horrible suffering; and that I feel that I must utter my cry of pain without putting it too plainly into words. If I did not, I should yield — —But you see nothing."

"And you will not make me happy!"

"Armand, I should die of sorrow the next day."

The General turned abruptly from her and went. But out in the street he brushed away the tears that he would not let fall.

The religious phase lasted for three months. At the end of that time the Duchess grew weary of vain repetitions; the Deity, bound hand and foot, was delivered up to her lover. Possibly she may have feared that by sheer dint of talking of eternity she might perpetuate his love in this world and the next. For her own sake, it must be believed that no man had touched her heart, or her conduct would be inexcusable. She was young; the time when men and women feel that they cannot afford to lose time or to quibble over their joys was still far off. She, no doubt, was on the verge not of first love, but of her first experience of the bliss of love. And from inexperience, for want of the painful lessons which would have taught her to value the treasure poured out at her feet, she was playing with it. Knowing nothing of the glory and rapture of the light, she was fain to stay in the shadow.

Armand was just beginning to understand this strange situation; he put his hope in the first word spoken by nature. Every evening, as he came away from Mme de Langeais', he told himself that no woman would accept the tenderest, most delicate proofs of a man's love during seven months, nor yield passively to the slighter demands of passion, only to cheat love at the last. He was waiting patiently for the sun to gain power, not doubting but that he should receive the earliest fruits. The married woman's hesitations and the religious scruples he could quite well understand. He even rejoiced over those battles. He mistook the Duchess's heartless coquetry for modesty; and he would not have had her otherwise. So he had loved to see her devising obstacles; was he not gradually triumphing over them? Did not every victory won swell the meagre sum of lovers' intimacies long denied, and at last conceded with every sign of love? Still, he had had such leisure to taste the full sweetness of every small successive conquest on which a lover feeds his love, that these had come to be matters of use and wont. So far as obstacles went, there were none now save his own awe of her; nothing else left between him and his desire save the whims of her who allowed him to call her Antoinette. So he made up his mind to demand more, to demand all. Embarrassed like a young lover who cannot dare to believe that his idol can stoop so low, he hesitated for a long time. He passed through the experience of terrible reactions within himself. A set purpose was annihilated by a word, and definite resolves died within him on the threshold. He despised himself for his weakness, and still his desire remained unuttered. Nevertheless, one evening, after sitting in gloomy melancholy, he brought out a fierce demand for his illegally legitimate rights. The Duchess had not to wait for her bond-slave's request to guess his desire. When was a man's desire a secret? And have not women an intuitive knowledge of the meaning of certain changes of countenance?

"What! you wish to be my friend no longer?" she broke in at the first words, and a divine red surging like new blood under the transparent skin, lent brightness to her eyes. "As a reward for my generosity, you would dishonor me? Just reflect a little. I myself have thought much over this; and I think always for us *both*. There is such a thing as a woman's loyalty, and we can no more fail in it than you can fail in honour. *I* cannot blind myself. If I am yours, how, in any sense, can I be M. de Langeais' wife? Can you require the sacrifice of my position, my rank, my whole life in return for a doubtful love that could not wait patiently for seven months? What! already you would rob me of my right to dispose of myself? No, no; you must not talk like this again. No, not another word. I will not, I cannot listen to you."

Mme de Langeais raised both hands to her head to push back the tufted curls from her hot forehead; she seemed very much excited.

"You come to a weak woman with your purpose definitely planned out. You say—'For a certain length of time she will talk to me of her husband, then of God, and then of the inevitable consequences. But I will use and abuse the ascendancy I shall gain over her; I will make myself indispensable; all the bonds of habit, all the misconstructions of outsiders, will make for me; and at length, when our *liaison* is taken for granted by all the world, I shall be this woman's master.' — Now, be frank; these are your thoughts! Oh! you calculate, and you say that you love. Shame on you! You are enamoured? Ah! that I well believe! You wish to possess me, to have me for your mistress, that is all! Very well then, No! The *Duchesse de Langeais* will not descend so far. Simple *bourgeoises* may be the victims of your treachery—I, never! Nothing gives me assurance of your love. You speak of my beauty; I may lose every trace of it in six months, like the dear Princess, my neighbour. You are captivated by my wit, my grace. Great Heavens! you would soon grow used to them and to the pleasures of possession. Have not the little concessions that I was weak enough to make come to be a matter of course in the last few months? Some day, when ruin comes, you will give me no reason for the change in you beyond a curt, 'I have ceased to care for you.' — Then, rank and fortune and honour and all that was the Duchesse de Langeais will be swallowed up in one disappointed hope. I shall have children to bear witness to my shame, and — —" With an involuntary gesture she interrupted herself, and continued: "But I am too good-natured to explain all this to you when you know it better than I. Come! let us stay as we are. I am only too fortunate in that I can still break these bonds which you think so strong. Is there anything so very heroic in coming to the Hotel de Langeais to spend an evening with a woman whose prattle amuses you?—a woman whom you take for a plaything? Why, half a dozen young coxcombs come here just as regularly every afternoon between three and five. They, too, are very generous, I am to suppose? I make fun of them; they stand my petulance and insolence pretty quietly, and make me laugh; but as for you, I give all the treasures of my soul to you, and you wish to ruin me, you try my patience in endless ways. Hush, that will do, that will do," she continued, seeing that he was about to speak, "you have no heart, no soul, no delicacy. I know what you want to tell me. Very well, then—yes. I would rather you should take me for a cold, insensible woman, with no devotion in her composition, no heart even, than be taken by everybody else for a vulgar person, and be condemned to your so-called pleasures, of which you would most certainly tire, and to everlasting punishment for it afterwards. Your selfish love is not worth so many sacrifices...."

The words give but a very inadequate idea of the discourse which the Duchess trilled out with the quick volubility of a bird-organ. Nor, truly, was there anything to prevent her from talking on for some time to come, for poor Armand's only reply to the torrent of flute notes was a silence filled with cruelly painful thoughts. He was just beginning to see that this woman was playing with him; he divined instinctively that a devoted love, a responsive love, does not reason and count the consequences in this way. Then, as he heard her reproach him with detestable motives, he felt something like shame as he remembered that unconsciously he had made those very calculations. With angelic honesty of purpose, he looked within, and self-examination found nothing but selfishness in all his thoughts and motives, in the answers which he framed and could not utter. He was self-convicted. In his despair he longed to fling himself from the window. The egoism of it was intolerable.

What indeed can a man say when a woman will not believe in love?—Let me prove how much I love you.—The *I* is always there.

The heroes of the boudoir, in such circumstances, can follow the example of the primitive logician who preceded the Pyrrhonists and denied movement. Montriveau was not equal to this feat. With all his audacity, he lacked this precise kind which never deserts an adept in the formulas of feminine algebra. If so many women, and even the best of women, fall a prey to a kind of expert to whom the vulgar give a grosser name, it is perhaps because the said experts are great *provers*, and love, in spite of its delicious poetry of sentiment, requires a little more geometry than people are wont to think.

Now the Duchess and Montriveau were alike in this—they were both equally unversed in love lore. The lady's knowledge of theory was but scanty; in practice she knew nothing whatever; she felt nothing, and reflected over everything. Montriveau had had but little experience, was absolutely ignorant of theory, and felt too much to reflect at all. Both therefore were enduring the consequences of the singular situation. At that supreme moment the myriad thoughts in his mind might have been reduced to the formula— "Submit to be mine——" words which seem horribly selfish to a woman for whom they awaken no memories, recall no ideas. Something nevertheless he must say. And what was more, though her barbed shafts had set his blood tingling, though the short phrases that she discharged at him one by one were very keen and sharp and cold, he must control himself lest he should lose all by an outbreak of anger.

"Mme la Duchesse, I am in despair that God should have invented no way for a woman to confirm the gift of her heart save by adding the gift of her person. The high value which you yourself put upon the gift teaches me that I cannot attach less importance to it. If you have given me your inmost self and your whole heart, as you tell me, what can the rest matter? And besides, if my happiness means so painful a sacrifice, let us say no more about it. But you must pardon a man of spirit if he feels humiliated at being taken for a spaniel."

The tone in which the last remark was uttered might perhaps have frightened another woman; but when the wearer of a petticoat has allowed herself to be addressed as a Divinity, and thereby set herself above all other mortals, no power on earth can be so haughty.

"M. le Marquis, I am in despair that God should not have invented some nobler way for a man to confirm the gift of his heart than by the manifestation of prodigiously vulgar desires. We become bond-slaves when we give ourselves body and soul, but a man is bound to nothing by accepting the gift. Who will assure me that love will last? The very love that I might show for you at every moment, the better to keep your love, might serve you as a reason for deserting me. I have no wish to be a second edition of Mme de Beauseant. Who can ever know what it is that keeps you beside us? Our persistent coldness of heart is the cause of an unfailing passion in some of you; other men ask for an untiring devotion, to be idolized at every moment; some for gentleness, others for tyranny. No woman in this world as yet has really read the riddle of man's heart."

There was a pause. When she spoke again it was in a different tone.

"After all, my friend, you cannot prevent a woman from trembling at the question, 'Will this love last always?' Hard though my words may be, the dread of losing you puts them into my mouth. Oh, me! it is not I who speaks, dear, it is reason; and how should anyone so mad as I be reasonable? In truth, I am nothing of the sort."

The poignant irony of her answer had changed before the end into the most musical accents in which a woman could find utterance for ingenuous love. To listen to her words was to pass in a moment from martyrdom to heaven. Montriveau grew pale; and for the first time in his life, he fell on his knees before a woman. He kissed the Duchess's skirt hem, her knees, her feet; but for the credit of the Faubourg Saint-Germain it is necessary to respect the mysteries of its boudoirs, where many are fain to take the utmost that Love can give without giving proof of love in return.

The Duchess thought herself generous when she suffered herself to be adored. But Montriveau was in a wild frenzy of joy over her complete surrender of the position.

"Dear Antoinette," he cried. "Yes, you are right; I will not have you doubt any longer. I too am trembling at this moment—lest the angel of my life should leave me; I wish I could invent some tie that might bind us to each other irrevocably."

"Ah!" she said, under her breath, "so I was right, you see."

"Let me say all that I have to say; I will scatter all your fears with a word. Listen! if I deserted you, I should deserve to die a thousand deaths. Be wholly mine, and I will give you the right to kill me if I am false. I myself will write a letter explaining certain reasons for taking my own life; I will make my final arrangements, in short. You shall have the letter in your keeping; in the eye of the law it will be a sufficient explanation of my death. You can avenge yourself, and fear nothing from God or men."

"What good would the letter be to me? What would life be if I had lost your love? If I wished to kill you, should I not be ready to follow? No; thank you for the thought, but I do not want the letter. Should I not begin to dread that you were faithful to me through fear? And if a man knows that he must risk his life for a stolen pleasure, might it not seem more tempting? Armand, the thing I ask of you is the one hard thing to do."

"Then what is it that you wish?"

"Your obedience and my liberty."

"Ah, God!" cried he, "I am a child."

"A wayward, much spoilt child," she said, stroking the thick hair, for his head still lay on her knee. "Ah! and loved far more than he believes, and yet he is very disobedient. Why not stay as we are? Why not sacrifice to me the desires that hurt me? Why not take what I can give, when it is all that I can honestly grant? Are you not happy?"

"Oh yes, I am happy when I have not a doubt left. Antoinette, doubt in love is a kind of death, is it not?"

In a moment he showed himself as he was, as all men are under the influence of that hot fever; he grew eloquent, insinuating. And the Duchess tasted the pleasures which she reconciled with her conscience by some private, Jesuitical ukase of her own; Armand's love gave her a thrill of cerebral excitement which custom made as necessary to her as society, or the Opera. To feel that she was adored by this man, who rose above other men, whose character frightened her; to treat him like a child; to play with him as Poppaea played with Nero—many women, like the wives of King Henry VIII, have paid for such a perilous delight with all the blood in their veins. Grim presentiment! Even as she surrendered the delicate, pale, gold curls to his touch, and felt the close pressure of his hand, the little hand of a man whose greatness she could not mistake; even as she herself played with his dark, thick locks, in that boudoir where she reigned a queen, the Duchess would say to herself:

"This man is capable of killing me if he once finds out that I am playing with him."

Armand de Montriveau stayed with her till two o'clock in the morning. From that moment this woman, whom he loved, was neither a duchess nor a Navarreins; Antoinette, in her disguises, had gone so far as to appear to be a woman. On that most blissful evening, the sweetest prelude ever played by a Parisienne to what the world calls "a slip"; in spite of all her affectations of a coyness which she did not feel, the General saw all maidenly beauty in her. He had some excuse for believing that so many storms of caprice had been but clouds covering a heavenly soul; that these must be lifted one by one like the veils that hid her divine loveliness. The Duchess became, for him, the most simple and girlish mistress; she was the one woman in the world for him; and he went away quite happy in that at last he had brought her to give him such pledges of love, that it seemed to him impossible but that he should be but her husband henceforth in secret, her choice sanctioned by Heaven.

Armand went slowly home, turning this thought in his mind with the impartiality of a man who is conscious of all the responsibilities that love lays on him while he tastes the sweetness of its joys. He went along the Quais to see the widest possible space of sky; his heart had grown in him; he would fain have had the bounds of the firmament and of earth enlarged. It seemed to him that his lungs drew an ampler breath. In the course of his self-examination, as he walked, he vowed to love this woman so devoutly, that every day of her life she should find absolution for her sins against society in unfailing happiness. Sweet stirrings of life when life is at the full! The man that is strong enough to steep his soul in the colour of one emotion, feels infinite joy as glimpses open out for him of an ardent lifetime that knows no diminution of passion to the end; even so it is permitted to certain mystics, in ecstasy, to behold the Light of God. Love would be naught without the belief that it would last forever; love grows great through constancy. It was thus that, wholly absorbed by his happiness, Montriveau understood passion.

"We belong to each other forever!"

The thought was like a talisman fulfilling the wishes of his life. He did not ask whether the Duchess might not change, whether her love might not last. No, for he had faith. Without that virtue there is no future for Christianity, and perhaps it is even more necessary to society. A conception of life as feeling occurred to him for the first time; hitherto he had lived by action, the most strenuous exertion of human energies, the physical devotion, as it may be called, of the soldier.

Next day M. de Montriveau went early in the direction of the Faubourg Saint-Germain. He had made an appointment at a house not far from the Hotel de Langeais; and the business over, he went thither as if to his own home. The General's companion chanced to be a man for whom he felt a kind of repulsion whenever he met him in other houses. This was the Marquis de Ronquerolles, whose reputation had grown so great in Paris boudoirs. He was witty, clever, and what was more—courageous; he set the fashion to all the young men in Paris. As a man of gallantry, his success and experience were equally matters of envy; and neither fortune nor birth was wanting in his case, qualifications which add such lustre in Paris to a reputation as a leader of fashion.

"Where are you going?" asked M. de Ronquerolles.

"To Mme de Langeais'."

"Ah, true. I forgot that you had allowed her to lime(sp) you. You are wasting your affections on her when they might be much better employed elsewhere. I could have told you of half a score of women in the financial world, any one of them a thousand times better worth your while than that titled courtesan, who does with her brains what less artificial women do with— —"

"What is this, my dear fellow?" Armand broke in. "The Duchess is an angel of innocence."

Ronquerolles began to laugh.

"Things being thus, dear boy," said he, "it is my duty to enlighten you. Just a word; there is no harm in it between ourselves. Has the Duchess surrendered? If so, I have nothing more to say. Come, give me your confidence. There is no occasion to waste your time in grafting your great nature on that unthankful stock, when all your hopes and cultivation will come to nothing."

Armand ingenuously made a kind of general report of his position, enumerating with much minuteness the slender rights so hardly won. Ronquerolles burst into a peal of laughter so heartless, that it would have cost any other man his life. But from their manner of speaking and looking at each other during that colloquy beneath the wall, in a corner almost as remote from intrusion as the desert itself, it was easy to imagine the friendship between the two men knew no bounds, and that no power on earth could estrange them.

"My dear Armand, why did you not tell me that the Duchess was a puzzle to you? I would have given you a little advice which might have brought your flirtation properly through. You must know, to begin with, that the women of our Faubourg, like any other women, love to steep themselves in love; but they have a mind to possess and not to be possessed. They have made a sort of compromise with human nature. The code of their parish gives them a pretty wide latitude short of the last transgression. The sweets enjoyed by this fair Duchess of yours are so many venial sins to be washed away in the waters of penitence. But if you had the impertinence to ask in earnest for the moral sin to which naturally you are sure to attach the highest importance, you would see the deep disdain with which the door of the boudoir and the house would be incontinently shut upon you. The tender Antoinette would dismiss everything from her memory; you would be less than a cipher for her. She would wipe away your kisses, my dear friend, as indifferently as she would perform her ablutions. She would sponge love from her cheeks as she washes off rouge. We know women of that sort—the thorough-bred Parisienne. Have you ever noticed a grisette tripping along the street? Her face is as good as a picture. A pretty cap, fresh cheeks, trim hair, a guileful smile, and the rest of her almost neglected. Is not this true to the life? Well, that is the Parisienne. She knows that her face is all that will be seen, so she devotes all her care, finery, and vanity to her head. The Duchess is the same; the head is everything with her. She can only feel through her intellect, her heart lies in her brain, she is a sort of intellectual epicure, she has a head-voice. We call that kind of poor creature a Lais of the intellect. You have been taken in like a boy. If you doubt it, you can have proof of it tonight, this morning, this instant. Go up to her, try the demand as an experiment, insist peremptorily if it is refused. You might set about it like the late Marechal de Richelieu, and get nothing for your pains."

Armand was dumb with amazement.

"Has your desire reached the point of infatuation?"

"I want her at any cost!" Montriveau cried out despairingly.

"Very well. Now, look here. Be as inexorable as she is herself. Try to humiliate her, to sting her vanity. Do *not* try to move her heart, nor her soul, but the woman's nerves and temperament, for she is both nervous and lymphatic. If you can once awaken desire in her, you are safe. But you must drop these romantic boyish notions of yours. If when once you have her in your eagle's talons you yield a point or draw back, if you so much as stir an eyelid, if she thinks that she can regain her ascendancy over you, she will slip out of your clutches like a fish, and you will never catch her again. Be as inflexible as law.

80

Show no more charity than the headsman. Hit hard, and then hit again. Strike and keep on striking as if you were giving her the knout. Duchesses are made of hard stuff, my dear Armand; there is a sort of feminine nature that is only softened by repeated blows; and as suffering develops a heart in women of that sort, so it is a work of charity not to spare the rod. Do you persevere. Ah! when pain has thoroughly relaxed those nerves and softened the fibres that you take to be so pliant and yielding; when a shriveled heart has learned to expand and contract and to beat under this discipline; when the brain has capitulated—then, perhaps, passion may enter among the steel springs of this machinery that turns out tears and affectations and languors and melting phrases; then you shall see a most magnificent conflagration (always supposing that the chimney takes fire). The steel feminine system will glow red-hot like iron in the forge; that kind of heat lasts longer than any other, and the glow of it may possibly turn to love.

"Still," he continued, "I have my doubts. And, after all, is it worth while to take so much trouble with the Duchess? Between ourselves a man of my stamp ought first to take her in hand and break her in; I would make a charming woman of her; she is a thoroughbred; whereas, you two left to yourselves will never get beyond the A B C. But you are in love with her, and just now you might not perhaps share my views on this subject——. A pleasant time to you, my children," added Ronquerolles, after a pause. Then with a laugh: "I have decided myself for facile beauties; they are tender, at any rate, the natural woman appears in their love without any of your social seasonings. A woman that haggles over herself, my poor boy, and only means to inspire love! Well, have her like an extra horse—for show. The match between the sofa and confessional, black and white, queen and knight, conscientious scruples and pleasure, is an uncommonly amusing game of chess. And if a man knows the game, let him be never so little of a rake, he wins in three moves. Now, if I undertook a woman of that sort, I should start with the deliberate purpose of——" His voice sank to a whisper over the last words in Armand's ear, and he went before there was time to reply.

As for Montriveau, he sprang at a bound across the courtyard of the Hotel de Langeais, went unannounced up the stairs straight to the Duchess's bedroom.

"This is an unheard-of thing," she said, hastily wrapping her dressing-gown about her. "Armand! this is abominable of you! Come, leave the room, I beg. Just go out of the room, and go at once. Wait for me in the drawing-room.—Come now!"

"Dear angel, has a plighted lover no privilege whatsoever?"

"But, monsieur, it is in the worst possible taste of a plighted lover or a wedded husband to break in like this upon his wife."

He came up to the Duchess, took her in his arms, and held her tightly to him.

"Forgive, dear Antoinette; but a host of horrid doubts are fermenting in my heart."

"*Doubts*? Fie!—Oh, fie on you!"

"Doubts all but justified. If you loved me, would you make this quarrel? Would you not be glad to see me? Would you not have felt a something stir in your heart? For I, that am not a woman, feel a thrill in my inmost self at the mere sound of your voice. Often in a ballroom a longing has come upon me to spring to your side and put my arms about your neck."

"Oh! if you have doubts of me so long as I am not ready to spring to your arms before all the world, I shall be doubted all my life long, I suppose. Why, Othello was a mere child compared with you!"

"Ah!" he cried despairingly, "you have no love for me— —"

"Admit, at any rate, that at this moment you are not lovable."

"Then I have still to find favour in your sight?"

"Oh, I should think so. Come," added she, "with a little imperious air, go out of the room, leave me. I am not like you; I wish always to find favour in your eyes."

Never woman better understood the art of putting charm into insolence, and does not the charm double the effect? is it not enough to infuriate the coolest of men? There was a sort of untrammeled freedom about Mme de Langeais; a something in her eyes, her voice, her attitude, which is never seen in a woman who loves when she stands face to face with him at the mere sight of whom her heart must needs begin to beat. The Marquis de Ronquerolles' counsels had cured Armand of sheepishness; and further, there came to his aid that rapid power of intuition which passion will develop at moments in the least wise among mortals, while a great man at such a time possesses it to the full. He guessed the terrible truth revealed by the Duchess's nonchalance, and his heart swelled with the storm like a lake rising in flood.

"If you told me the truth yesterday, be mine, dear Antoinette," he cried; "you shall——"

"In the first place," said she composedly, thrusting him back as he came nearer—"in the first place, you are not to compromise me. My woman might overhear you. Respect me, I beg of you. Your familiarity is all very well in my boudoir in an evening; here it is quite different. Besides, what may your 'you shall' mean? 'You shall.' No one as yet has ever used that word to me. It is quite ridiculous, it seems to me, absolutely ridiculous."

"Will you surrender nothing to me on this point?"

"Oh! do you call a woman's right to dispose of herself a 'point?' A capital point indeed; you will permit me to be entirely my own mistress on that 'point.'"

"And how if, believing in your promises to me, I should absolutely require it?"

"Oh! then you would prove that I made the greatest possible mistake when I made you a promise of any kind; and I should beg you to leave me in peace."

The General's face grew white; he was about to spring to her side, when Mme de Langeais rang the bell, the maid appeared, and, smiling with a mocking grace, the Duchess added, "Be so good as to return when I am visible."

Then Montriveau felt the hardness of a woman as cold and keen as a steel blade; she was crushing in her scorn. In one moment she had snapped the bonds which held firm only for her lover. She had read

Armand's intention in his face, and held that the moment had come for teaching the Imperial soldier his lesson. He was to be made to feel that though duchesses may lend themselves to love, they do not give themselves, and that the conquest of one of them would prove a harder matter than the conquest of Europe.

"Madame," returned Armand, "I have not time to wait. I am a spoilt child, as you told me yourself. When I seriously resolve to have that of which we have been speaking, I shall have it."

"You will have it?" queried she, and there was a trace of surprise in her loftiness.

"I shall have it."

"Oh! you would do me a great pleasure by 'resolving' to have it. For curiosity's sake, I should be delighted to know how you would set about it— —"

"I am delighted to put a new interest into your life," interrupted Montriveau, breaking into a laugh which dismayed the Duchess. "Will you permit me to take you to the ball tonight?"

"A thousand thanks. M. de Marsay has been beforehand with you. I gave him my promise."

Montriveau bowed gravely and went.

"So Ronquerolles was right," thought he, "and now for a game of chess."

Thenceforward he hid his agitation by complete composure. No man is strong enough to bear such sudden alternations from the height of happiness to the depths of wretchedness. So he had caught a glimpse of happy life the better to feel the emptiness of his previous existence? There was a terrible storm within him; but he had learned to endure, and bore the shock of tumultuous thoughts as a granite cliff stands out against the surge of an angry sea.

"I could say nothing. When I am with her my wits desert me. She does not know how vile and contemptible she is. Nobody has ventured to bring her face to face with herself. She has played with many a man, no doubt; I will avenge them all."

For the first time, it may be, in a man's heart, revenge and love were blended so equally that Montriveau himself could not know whether love or revenge would carry all before it. That very evening he went to the ball at which he was sure of seeing the Duchesse de Langeais, and almost despaired of reaching her heart. He inclined to think that there was something diabolical about this woman, who was gracious to him and radiant with charming smiles; probably because she had no wish to allow the world to think that she had compromised herself with M. de Montriveau. Coolness on both sides is a sign of love; but so long as the Duchess was the same as ever, while the Marquis looked sullen and morose, was it not plain that she had conceded nothing? Onlookers know the rejected lover by various signs and tokens; they never mistake the genuine symptoms for a coolness such as some women command their adorers to feign, in the hope of concealing their love. Everyone laughed at Montriveau; and he, having omitted to consult his cornac, was abstracted and ill at ease. M. de Ronquerolles would very likely have bidden him compromise the Duchess by responding to her show of friendliness by passionate demonstrations; but as it was, Armand de Montriveau came away from the ball, loathing human nature, and even then scarcely ready to believe in such complete depravity.

"If there is no executioner for such crimes," he said, as he looked up at the lighted windows of the ballroom where the most enchanting women in Paris were dancing, laughing, and chatting, "I will take you by the nape of the neck, Mme la Duchesse, and make you feel something that bites more deeply than the knife in the Place de la Greve. Steel against steel; we shall see which heart will leave the deeper mark."

For a week or so Mme de Langeais hoped to see the Marquis de Montriveau again; but he contented himself with sending his card every morning to the Hotel de Langeais. The Duchess could not help shuddering each time that the card was brought in, and a dim foreboding crossed her mind, but the thought was vague as a presentiment of disaster. When her eyes fell on the name, it seemed to her that she felt the touch of the implacable man's strong hand in her hair; sometimes the words seemed like a prognostication of a vengeance which her lively intellect invented in the most shocking forms. She had studied him too well not to dread him. Would he murder her, she wondered? Would that bull-necked man dash out her vitals by flinging her over his head? Would he trample her body under his feet? When, where, and how would he get her into his power? Would he make her suffer very much, and what kind of pain would he inflict? She repented of her conduct. There were hours when, if he had come, she would have gone to his arms in complete self-surrender.

Every night before she slept she saw Montriveau's face; every night it wore a different aspect. Sometimes she saw his bitter smile, sometimes the Jovelike knitting of the brows; or his leonine look, or some disdainful movement of the shoulders made him terrible for her. Next day the card seemed stained with blood. The name of Montriveau stirred her now as the presence of the fiery, stubborn, exacting lover had never done. Her apprehensions gathered strength in the silence. She was forced, without aid from without, to face the thought of a hideous duel of which she could not speak. Her proud hard nature was more responsive to thrills of hate than it had ever been to the caresses of love. Ah! if the General could but have seen her, as she sat with her forehead drawn into folds between her brows; immersed in bitter thoughts in that boudoir where he had enjoyed such happy moments, he might perhaps have conceived high hopes. Of all human passions, is not pride alone incapable of engendering anything base? Mme de Langeais kept her thoughts to herself, but is it not permissible to suppose that M. de Montriveau was no longer indifferent to her? And has not a man gained ground immensely when a woman thinks about him? He is bound to make progress with her either one way or the other afterwards.

Put any feminine creature under the feet of a furious horse or other fearsome beast; she will certainly drop on her knees and look for death; but if the brute shows a milder mood and does not utterly slay her, she will love the horse, lion, bull, or what not, and will speak of him quite at her ease. The Duchess felt that she was under the lion's paws; she quaked, but she did not hate him.

The man and woman thus singularly placed with regard to each other met three times in society during the course of that week. Each time, in reply to coquettish questioning glances, the Duchess received a respectful bow, and smiles tinged with such savage irony, that all her apprehensions over the card in the morning were revived at night. Our lives are simply such as our feelings shape them for us; and the feelings of these two had hollowed out a great gulf between them.

The Comtesse de Serizy, the Marquis de Ronquerolles' sister, gave a great ball at the beginning of the following week, and Mme de Langeais was sure to go to it. Armand was the first person whom the Duchess saw when she came into the room, and this time Armand was looking out for her, or so she thought at least. The two exchanged a look, and suddenly the woman felt a cold perspiration break from every pore. She had thought all along that Montriveau was capable of taking reprisals in some unheard-of way proportioned to their condition, and now the revenge had been discovered, it was ready, heated, and boiling. Lightnings flashed from the foiled lover's eyes, his face was radiant with exultant vengeance. And the Duchess? Her eyes were haggard in spite of her resolution to be cool and insolent. She went to take her place beside the Comtesse de Serizy, who could not help exclaiming, "Dear Antoinette! what is the matter with you? You are enough to frighten one."

"I shall be all right after a quadrille," she answered, giving a hand to a young man who came up at that moment.

Mme de Langeais waltzed that evening with a sort of excitement and transport which redoubled Montriveau's lowering looks. He stood in front of the line of spectators, who were amusing themselves by looking on. Every time that *she* came past him, his eyes darted down upon her eddying face; he might have been a tiger with the prey in his grasp. The waltz came to an end, Mme de Langeais went back to her place beside the Countess, and Montriveau never took his eyes off her, talking all the while with a stranger.

"One of the things that struck me most on the journey," he was saying (and the Duchess listened with all her ears), "was the remark which the man makes at Westminster when you are shown the axe with which a man in a mask cut off Charles the First's head, so they tell you. The King made it first of all to some inquisitive person, and they repeat it still in memory of him."

"What does the man say?" asked Mme de Serizy.

"'Do not touch the axe!'" replied Montriveau, and there was menace in the sound of his voice.

"Really, my Lord Marquis," said Mme de Langeais, "you tell this old story that everybody knows if they have been to London, and look at my neck in such a melodramatic way that you seem to me to have an axe in your hand."

The Duchess was in a cold sweat, but nevertheless she laughed as she spoke the last words.

"But circumstances give the story a quite new application," returned he.

"How so; pray tell me, for pity's sake?"

"In this way, madame—you have touched the axe," said Montriveau, lowering his voice.

"What an enchanting prophecy!" returned she, smiling with assumed grace. "And when is my head to fall?"

"I have no wish to see that pretty head of yours cut off. I only fear some great misfortune for you. If your head were clipped close, would you feel no regrets for the dainty golden hair that you turn to such good account?"

"There are those for whom a woman would love to make such a sacrifice; even if, as often happens, it is for the sake of a man who cannot make allowances for an outbreak of temper."

"Quite so. Well, and if some wag were to spoil your beauty on a sudden by some chemical process, and you, who are but eighteen for us, were to be a hundred years old?"

"Why, the smallpox is our Battle of Waterloo, monsieur," she interrupted. "After it is over we find out those who love us sincerely."

"Would you not regret the lovely face that?"

"Oh! indeed I should, but less for my own sake than for the sake of someone else whose delight it might have been. And, after all, if I were loved, always loved, and truly loved, what would my beauty matter to me? — What do you say, Clara?"

"It is a dangerous speculation," replied Mme de Serizy.

"Is it permissible to ask His Majesty the King of Sorcerers when I made the mistake of touching the axe, since I have not been to London as yet? — —"

"*Not so,*" he answered in English, with a burst of ironical laughter.

"And when will the punishment begin?"

At this Montriveau coolly took out his watch, and ascertained the hour with a truly appalling air of conviction.

"A dreadful misfortune will befall you before this day is out."

"I am not a child to be easily frightened, or rather, I am a child ignorant of danger," said the Duchess. "I shall dance now without fear on the edge of the precipice."

"I am delighted to know that you have so much strength of character," he answered, as he watched her go to take her place in a square dance.

But the Duchess, in spite of her apparent contempt for Armand's dark prophecies, was really frightened. Her late lover's presence weighed upon her morally and physically with a sense of oppression that scarcely ceased when he left the ballroom. And yet when she had drawn freer breath, and enjoyed the relief for a moment, she found herself regretting the sensation of dread, so greedy of extreme sensations is the feminine nature. The regret was not love, but it was certainly akin to other feelings which prepare the way for love. And then — as if the impression which Montriveau had made upon her were suddenly revived — she recollected his air of conviction as he took out his watch, and in a sudden spasm of dread she went out.

By this time it was about midnight. One of her servants, waiting with her pelisse, went down to order her carriage. On her way home she fell naturally enough to musing over M. de Montriveau's prediction. Arrived in her own courtyard, as she supposed, she entered a vestibule almost like that of her own hotel, and suddenly saw that the staircase was different. She was in a strange house. Turning to call her servants, she was attacked by several men, who rapidly flung a handkerchief over her mouth, bound her hand and foot, and carried her off. She shrieked aloud.

"Madame, our orders are to kill you if you scream," a voice said in her ear.

So great was the Duchess's terror, that she could never recollect how nor by whom she was transported. When she came to herself, she was lying on a couch in a bachelor's lodging, her hands and feet tied with silken cords. In spite of herself, she shrieked aloud as she looked round and met Armand de Montriveau's eyes. He was sitting in his dressing-gown, quietly smoking a cigar in his armchair.

"Do not cry out, Mme la Duchesse," he said, coolly taking the cigar out of his mouth; "I have a headache. Besides, I will untie you. But listen attentively to what I have the honour to say to you."

Very carefully he untied the knots that bound her feet.

"What would be the use of calling out? Nobody can hear your cries. You are too well bred to make any unnecessary fuss. If you do not stay quietly, if you insist upon a struggle with me, I shall tie your hands and feet again. All things considered, I think that you have self-respect enough to stay on this sofa as if you were lying on your own at home; cold as ever, if you will. You have made me shed many tears on this couch, tears that I hid from all other eyes."

While Montriveau was speaking, the Duchess glanced about her; it was a woman's glance, a stolen look that saw all things and seemed to see nothing. She was much pleased with the room. It was rather like a monk's cell. The man's character and thoughts seemed to pervade it. No decoration of any kind broke the grey painted surface of the walls. A green carpet covered the floor. A black sofa, a table littered with papers, two big easy-chairs, a chest of drawers with an alarum clock by way of ornament, a very low bedstead with a coverlet flung over it—a red cloth with a black key border—all these things made part of a whole that told of a life reduced to its simplest terms. A triple candle-sconce of Egyptian design on the chimney-piece recalled the vast spaces of the desert and Montriveau's long wanderings; a huge sphinx-claw stood out beneath the folds of stuff at the bed-foot; and just beyond, a green curtain with a black and scarlet border was suspended by large rings from a spear handle above a door near one corner of the room. The other door by which the band had entered was likewise curtained, but the drapery hung from an ordinary curtain-rod. As the Duchess finally noted that the pattern was the same on both, she saw that the door at the bed-foot stood open; gleams of ruddy light from the room beyond flickered below the fringed border. Naturally, the ominous light roused her curiosity; she fancied she could distinguish strange shapes in the shadows; but as it did not occur to her at the time that danger could come from that quarter, she tried to gratify a more ardent curiosity.

"Monsieur, if it is not indiscreet, may I ask what you mean to do with me?" The insolence and irony of the tone stung through the words. The Duchess quite believed that she read extravagant love in Montriveau's speech. He had carried her off; was not that in itself an acknowledgment of her power?

"Nothing whatever, madame," he returned, gracefully puffing the last whiff of cigar smoke. "You will remain here for a short time. First of all, I should like to explain to you what you are, and what I am. I cannot put my thoughts into words whilst you are twisting on the sofa in your boudoir; and besides, in your own house you take offence at the slightest hint, you ring the bell, make an outcry, and turn your lover out at the door as if he were the basest of wretches. Here my mind is unfettered. Here nobody can turn me out. Here you shall be my victim for a few seconds, and you are going to be so exceedingly kind as to listen to me. You need fear nothing. I did not carry you off to insult you, nor yet to take by force what you refused to grant of your own will to my unworthiness. I could not stoop so low. You possibly think of outrage; for myself, I have no such thoughts."

He flung his cigar coolly into the fire.

"The smoke is unpleasant to you, no doubt, madame?" he said, and rising at once, he took a chafing-dish from the hearth, burnt perfumes, and purified the air. The Duchess's astonishment was only equaled by her humiliation. She was in this man's power; and he would not abuse his power. The eyes in which love had once blazed like flame were now quiet and steady as stars. She trembled. Her dread of Armand was increased by a nightmare sensation of restlessness and utter inability to move; she felt as if she were turned to stone. She lay passive in the grip of fear. She thought she saw the light behind the curtains grow to a blaze, as if blown up by a pair of bellows; in another moment the gleams of flame grew brighter, and she fancied that three masked figures suddenly flashed out; but the terrible vision disappeared so swiftly that she took it for an optical delusion.

"Madame," Armand continued with cold contempt, "one minute, just one minute is enough for me, and you shall feel it afterwards at every moment throughout your lifetime, the one eternity over which I have power. I am not God. Listen carefully to me," he continued, pausing to add solemnity to his words. "Love will always come at your call. You have boundless power over men: but remember that once you called love, and love came to you; love as pure and true-hearted as may be on earth, and as reverent as it was passionate; fond as a devoted woman's, as a mother's love; a love so great indeed, that it was past the bounds of reason. You played with it, and you committed a crime. Every woman has a right to refuse herself to love which she feels she cannot share; and if a man loves and cannot win love in return, he is not to be pitied, he has no right to complain. But with a semblance of love to attract an unfortunate creature cut off from all affection; to teach him to understand happiness to the full, only to snatch it from him; to rob him of his future of felicity; to slay his happiness not merely today, but as long as his life lasts, by poisoning every hour of it and every thought — this I call a fearful crime!"

"Monsieur — —"

"I cannot allow you to answer me yet. So listen to me still. In any case I have rights over you; but I only choose to exercise one — the right of the judge over the criminal, so that I may arouse your conscience. If you had no conscience left, I should not reproach you at all; but you are so young! You must feel some life still in your heart; or so I like to believe. While I think of you as depraved enough to do a wrong which the law does not punish, I do not think you so degraded that you cannot comprehend the full meaning of my words. I resume."

As he spoke the Duchess heard the smothered sound of a pair of bellows. Those mysterious figures which she had just seen were blowing up the fire, no doubt; the glow shone through the curtain. But Montriveau's lurid face was turned upon her; she could not choose but wait with a fast-beating heart and eyes fixed in a stare. However curious she felt, the heat in Armand's words interested her even more than the crackling of the mysterious flames.

"Madame," he went on after a pause, "if some poor wretch commits a murder in Paris, it is the executioner's duty, you know, to lay hands on him and stretch him on the plank, where murderers pay for their crimes with their heads. Then the newspapers inform everyone, rich and poor, so that the former are assured that they may sleep in peace, and the latter are warned that they must be on the watch if they would live. Well, you that are religious, and even a little of a bigot, may have masses said for such a man's soul. You both belong to the same family, but yours is the elder branch; and the elder branch may occupy high places in peace and live happily and without cares. Want or anger may drive your brother the convict to take a man's life; you have taken more, you have taken the joy out of a man's life, you have killed all that was best in his life—his dearest beliefs. The murderer simply lay in wait for his victim, and killed him reluctantly, and in fear of the scaffold; but *you* ...! You heaped up every sin that weakness can commit against strength that suspected no evil; you tamed a passive victim, the better to gnaw his heart out; you lured him with caresses; you left nothing undone that could set him dreaming, imagining, longing for the bliss of love. You asked innumerable sacrifices of him, only to refuse to make any in return. He should see the light indeed before you put out his eyes! It is wonderful how you found the heart to do it! Such villainies demand a display of resource quite above the comprehension of those bourgeoises whom you laugh at and despise. They can give and forgive; they know how to love and suffer. The grandeur of their devotion dwarfs us. Rising higher in the social scale, one finds just as much mud as at the lower end; but with this difference, at the upper end it is hard and gilded over.

"Yes, to find baseness in perfection, you must look for a noble bringing up, a great name, a fair woman, a duchess. You cannot fall

93

lower than the lowest unless you are set high above the rest of the world.—I express my thoughts badly; the wounds you dealt me are too painful as yet, but do not think that I complain. My words are not the expression of any hope for myself; there is no trace of bitterness in them. Know this, madame, for a certainty—I forgive you. My forgiveness is so complete that you need not feel in the least sorry that you came hither to find it against your will.... But you might take advantage of other hearts as child-like as my own, and it is my duty to spare them anguish. So you have inspired the thought of justice. Expiate your sin here on earth; God may perhaps forgive you; I wish that He may, but He is inexorable, and will strike."

The broken-spirited, broken-hearted woman looked up, her eyes filled with tears.

"Why do you cry? Be true to your nature. You could look on indifferently at the torture of a heart as you broke it. That will do, madame, do not cry. I cannot bear it any longer. Other men will tell you that you have given them life; as for myself, I tell you, with rapture, that you have given me blank extinction. Perhaps you guess that I am not my own, that I am bound to live for my friends, that from this time forth I must endure the cold chill of death, as well as the burden of life? Is it possible that there can be so much kindness in you? Are you like the desert tigress that licks the wounds she has inflicted?"

The Duchess burst out sobbing.

"Pray spare your tears, madame. If I believed in them at all, it would merely set me on my guard. Is this another of your artifices? or is it not? You have used so many with me; how can one think that there is any truth in you? Nothing that you do or say has any power now to move me. That is all I have to say."

Mme de Langeais rose to her feet, with a great dignity and humility in her bearing.

"You are right to treat me very hardly," she said, holding out a hand to the man who did not take it; "you have not spoken hardly enough; and I deserve this punishment."

"*I* punish you, madame! A man must love still, to punish, must he not? From me you must expect no feeling, nothing resembling it. If I chose, I might be accuser and judge in my cause, and pronounce and carry out the sentence. But I am about to fulfil a duty, not a desire of vengeance of any kind. The cruelest revenge of all, I think, is scorn of revenge when it is in our power to take it. Perhaps I shall be the minister of your pleasures; who knows? Perhaps from this time forth, as you gracefully wear the tokens of disgrace by which society marks out the criminal, you may perforce learn something of the convict's sense of honour. And then, you will love!"

The Duchess sat listening; her meekness was unfeigned; it was no coquettish device. When she spoke at last, it was after a silence.

"Armand," she began, "it seems to me that when I resisted love, I was obeying all the instincts of woman's modesty; I should not have looked for such reproaches from *you*. I was weak; you have turned all my weaknesses against me, and made so many crimes of them. How could you fail to understand that the curiosity of love might have carried me further than I ought to go; and that next morning I might be angry with myself, and wretched because I had gone too far? Alas! I sinned in ignorance. I was as sincere in my wrongdoing, I swear to you, as in my remorse. There was far more love for you in my severity than in my concessions. And besides, of what do you complain? I gave you my heart; that was not enough; you demanded, brutally, that I should give my person——"

"Brutally?" repeated Montriveau. But to himself he said, "If I once allow her to dispute over words, I am lost."

"Yes. You came to me as if I were one of those women. You showed none of the respect, none of the attentions of love. Had I not reason to reflect? Very well, I reflected. The unseemliness of your conduct is not inexcusable; love lay at the source of it; let me think so, and justify you to myself.—Well, Armand, this evening, even while you were prophesying evil, I felt convinced that there was happiness in store for us both. Yes, I put my faith in the noble, proud nature so often tested and proved." She bent lower. "And I was yours wholly," she murmured in his ear. "I felt a longing that I cannot express to give happiness to a man so violently tried by adversity. If I must have a master, my master should be a great man. As I felt conscious of my height, the less I cared to descend. I felt I could trust you, I saw a whole lifetime of love, while you were pointing to death.... Strength and kindness always go together. My friend, you are so strong, you will not be unkind to a helpless woman who loves you. If I was wrong, is there no way of obtaining forgiveness? No way of making reparation? Repentance is the charm of love; I should like to be very charming for you. How could I, alone among women, fail to know a woman's doubts and fears, the timidity that it is so natural to feel when you bind yourself for life, and know how easily a man snaps such ties? The bourgeoises, with whom you compared me just now, give themselves, but they struggle first. Very well—I struggled; but here I am!—Ah! God, he does not hear me!" she broke off, and wringing her hands, she cried out "But I love you! I am yours!" and fell at Armand's feet.

"Yours! yours! my one and only master!"

Armand tried to raise her.

"Madame, it is too late! Antoinette cannot save the Duchesse de Langeais. I cannot believe in either. Today you may give yourself; tomorrow, you may refuse. No power in earth or heaven can insure me the sweet constancy of love. All love's pledges lay in the past; and now nothing of that past exists."

The light behind the curtain blazed up so brightly, that the Duchess could not help turning her head; this time she distinctly saw the three masked figures.

"Armand," she said, "I would not wish to think ill of you. Why are those men there? What are you going to do to me?"

"Those men will be as silent as I myself with regard to the thing which is about to be done. Think of them simply as my hands and my heart. One of them is a surgeon——"

"A surgeon! Armand, my friend, of all things, suspense is the hardest to bear. Just speak; tell me if you wish for my life; I will give it to you, you shall not take it——"

"Then you did not understand me? Did I not speak just now of justice? To put an end to your misapprehensions," continued he, taking up a small steel object from the table, "I will now explain what I have decided with regard to you."

He held out a Lorraine cross, fastened to the tip of a steel rod.

"Two of my friends at this very moment are heating another cross, made on this pattern, red-hot. We are going to stamp it upon your forehead, here between the eyes, so that there will be no possibility of hiding the mark with diamonds, and so avoiding people's questions. In short, you shall bear on your forehead the brand of infamy which your brothers the convicts wear on their shoulders. The pain is a mere trifle, but I feared a nervous crisis of some kind, of resistance——"

"Resistance?" she cried, clapping her hands for joy. "Oh no, no! I would have the whole world here to see. Ah, my Armand, brand her quickly, this creature of yours; brand her with your mark as a poor little trifle belonging to you. You asked for pledges of my love; here they are all in one. Ah! for me there is nothing but mercy and forgiveness and eternal happiness in this revenge of yours. When you have marked this woman with your mark, when you set your crimson brand on her, your slave in soul, you can never afterwards abandon her, you will be mine for evermore? When you cut me off from my kind, you make yourself responsible for my happiness, or you prove yourself base; and I know that you are noble and great! Why, when a woman loves, the brand of love is burnt into her soul by her own will.—Come in, gentlemen! come in and brand her, this Duchesse de Langeais. She is M. de Montriveau's forever! Ah! come quickly, all of you, my forehead burns hotter than your fire!"

Armand turned his head sharply away lest he should see the Duchess kneeling, quivering with the throbbings of her heart. He said some word, and his three friends vanished.

The women of Paris salons know how one mirror reflects another. The Duchess, with every motive for reading the depths of Armand's heart, was all eyes; and Armand, all unsuspicious of the mirror, brushed away two tears as they fell. Her whole future lay in those two tears. When he turned round again to help her to rise, she was standing before him, sure of love. Her pulses must have throbbed fast when he spoke with the firmness she had known so well how to use of old while she played with him.

"I spare you, madame. All that has taken place shall be as if it had never been, you may believe me. But now, let us bid each other goodbye. I like to think that you were sincere in your coquetries on your sofa, sincere again in this outpouring of your heart. Good-bye. I feel that there is no faith in you left in me. You would torment me again; you would always be the Duchess, and — —But there, good-bye, we shall never understand each other.

"Now, what do you wish?" he continued, taking the tone of a master of the ceremonies—"to return home, or to go back to Mme de Serizy's ball? I have done all in my power to prevent any scandal. Neither your servants nor anyone else can possibly know what has passed between us in the last quarter of an hour. Your servants have no idea that you have left the ballroom; your carriage never left Mme de Serizy's courtyard; your brougham may likewise be found in the court of your own hotel. Where do you wish to be?"

"What do you counsel, Armand?"

"There is no Armand now, Mme la Duchesse. We are strangers to each other."

"Then take me to the ball," she said, still curious to put Armand's power to the test. "Thrust a soul that suffered in the world, and must always suffer there, if there is no happiness for her now, down into hell again. And yet, oh my friend, I love you as your bourgeoises love; I love you so that I could come to you and fling my arms about your neck before all the world if you asked it off me. The hateful world has not corrupted me. I am young at least, and I have grown younger still. I am a child, yes, your child, your new creature. Ah! do not drive me forth out of my Eden!"

Armand shook his head.

"Ah! let me take something with me, if I go, some little thing to wear tonight on my heart," she said, taking possession of Armand's glove, which she twisted into her handkerchief.

"No, I am *not* like all those depraved women. You do not know the world, and so you cannot know my worth. You shall know it now!

There are women who sell themselves for money; there are others to be gained by gifts, it is a vile world! Oh, I wish I were a simple bourgeoise, a working girl, if you would rather have a woman beneath you than a woman whose devotion is accompanied by high rank, as men count it. Oh, my Armand, there are noble, high, and chaste and pure natures among us; and then they are lovely indeed. I would have all nobleness that I might offer it all up to you. Misfortune willed that I should be a duchess; I would I were a royal princess, that my offering might be complete. I would be a grisette for you, and a queen for everyone besides."

He listened, damping his cigars with his lips.

"You will let me know when you wish to go," he said.

"But I should like to stay — —"

"That is another matter!"

"Stay, that was badly rolled," she cried, seizing on a cigar and devouring all that Armand's lips had touched.

"Do you smoke?"

"Oh, what would I not do to please you?"

"Very well. Go, madame."

"I will obey you," she answered, with tears in her eyes.

"You must be blindfolded; you must not see a glimpse of the way."

"I am ready, Armand," she said, bandaging her eyes.

"Can you see?"

"No."

Noiselessly he knelt before her.

"Ah! I can hear you!" she cried, with a little fond gesture, thinking that the pretence of harshness was over.

He made as if he would kiss her lips; she held up her face.

"You can see, madame."

"I am just a little bit curious."

"So you always deceive me?"

"Ah! take off this handkerchief, sir," she cried out, with the passion of a great generosity repelled with scorn, "lead me; I will not open my eyes."

Armand felt sure of her after that cry. He led the way; the Duchess nobly true to her word, was blind. But while Montriveau held her hand as a father might, and led her up and down flights of stairs, he was studying the throbbing pulses of this woman's heart so suddenly invaded by Love. Mme de Langeais, rejoicing in this power of speech, was glad to let him know all; but he was inflexible; his hand was passive in reply to the questionings of her hand.

At length, after some journey made together, Armand bade her go forward; the opening was doubtless narrow, for as she went she felt that his hand protected her dress. His care touched her; it was a revelation surely that there was a little love still left; yet it was in some sort a farewell, for Montriveau left her without a word. The air was warm; the Duchess, feeling the heat, opened her eyes, and found herself standing by the fire in the Comtesse de Serizy's boudoir.

She was alone. Her first thought was for her disordered toilette; in a moment she had adjusted her dress and restored her picturesque coiffure.

"Well, dear Antoinette, we have been looking for you everywhere." It was the Comtesse de Serizy who spoke as she opened the door.

"I came here to breathe," said the Duchess; "it is unbearably hot in the rooms."

"People thought that you had gone; but my brother Ronquerolles told me that your servants were waiting for you."

"I am tired out, dear, let me stay and rest here for a minute," and the Duchess sat down on the sofa.

"Why, what is the matter with you? You are shaking from head to foot!"

The Marquis de Ronquerolles came in.

100

"Mme la Duchesse, I was afraid that something might have happened. I have just come across your coachman, the man is as tipsy as all the Swiss in Switzerland."

The Duchess made no answer; she was looking round the room, at the chimney-piece and the tall mirrors, seeking the trace of an opening. Then with an extraordinary sensation she recollected that she was again in the midst of the gaiety of the ballroom after that terrific scene which had changed the whole course of her life. She began to shiver violently.

"M. de Montriveau's prophecy has shaken my nerves," she said. "It was a joke, but still I will see whether his axe from London will haunt me even in my sleep. So good-bye, dear.—Good-bye, M. le Marquis."

As she went through the rooms she was beset with inquiries and regrets. Her world seemed to have dwindled now that she, its queen, had fallen so low, was so diminished. And what, moreover, were these men compared with him whom she loved with all her heart; with the man grown great by all that she had lost in stature? The giant had regained the height that he had lost for a while, and she exaggerated it perhaps beyond measure. She looked, in spite of herself, at the servant who had attended her to the ball. He was fast asleep.

"Have you been here all the time?" she asked.

"Yes, madame."

As she took her seat in her carriage she saw, in fact, that her coachman was drunk—so drunk, that at any other time she would have been afraid; but after a great crisis in life, fear loses its appetite for common food. She reached home, at any rate, without accident; but even there she felt a change in herself, a new feeling that she could not shake off. For her, there was now but one man in the world; which is to say that henceforth she cared to shine for his sake alone.

While the physiologist can define love promptly by following out natural laws, the moralist finds a far more perplexing problem before him if he attempts to consider love in all its developments due to social conditions. Still, in spite of the heresies of the endless sects that divide the church of Love, there is one broad and trenchant line of difference in doctrine, a line that all the discussion in the world can never deflect. A rigid application of this line explains the nature of the crisis through which the Duchess, like most women, was to pass. Passion she knew, but she did not love as yet.

Love and passion are two different conditions which poets and men of the world, philosophers and fools, alike continually confound. Love implies a give and take, a certainty of bliss that nothing can change; it means so close a clinging of the heart, and an exchange of happiness so constant, that there is no room left for jealousy. Then possession is a means and not an end; unfaithfulness may give pain, but the bond is not less close; the soul is neither more nor less ardent or troubled, but happy at every moment; in short, the divine breath of desire spreading from end to end of the immensity of Time steeps it all for us in the selfsame hue; life takes the tint of the unclouded heaven. But Passion is the foreshadowing of Love, and of that Infinite to which all suffering souls aspire. Passion is a hope that may be cheated. Passion means both suffering and transition. Passion dies out when hope is dead. Men and women may pass through this experience many times without dishonor, for it is so natural to spring towards happiness; but there is only one love in a lifetime. All discussions of sentiment ever conducted on paper or by word of mouth may therefore be resumed by two questions—"Is it passion? Is it love?" So, since love comes into existence only through the intimate experience of the bliss which gives it lasting life, the Duchess was beneath the yoke of passion as yet; and as she knew the fierce tumult, the unconscious calculations, the fevered cravings, and all that is meant by that word *passion*—she suffered. Through all the trouble of her soul there rose eddying gusts of tempest, raised by vanity or self-love, or pride or a high spirit; for all these forms of egoism make common cause together.

She had said to this man, "I love you; I am yours!" Was it possible that the Duchesse de Langeais should have uttered those words—in vain? She must either be loved now or play her part of queen no longer. And then she felt the loneliness of the luxurious couch where pleasure had never yet set his glowing feet; and over and over again, while she tossed and writhed there, she said, "I want to be loved."

But the belief that she still had in herself gave her hope of success. The Duchess might be piqued, the vain Parisienne might be humiliated; but the woman saw glimpses of wedded happiness, and imagination, avenging the time lost for nature, took a delight in kindling the inextinguishable fire in her veins. She all but attained to the sensations of love; for amid her poignant doubt whether she was loved in return, she felt glad at heart to say to herself, "I love him!" As for her scruples, religion, and the world she could trample them under foot! Montriveau was her religion now. She spent the next day in a state of moral torpor, troubled by a physical unrest, which no words could express. She wrote letters and tore them all up, and invented a thousand impossible fancies.

When M. de Montriveau's usual hour arrived, she tried to think that he would come, and enjoyed the feeling of expectation. Her whole life was concentrated in the single sense of hearing. Sometimes she shut her eyes, straining her ears to listen through space, wishing that she could annihilate everything that lay between her and her lover, and so establish that perfect silence which sounds may traverse from afar. In her tense self-concentration, the ticking of the clock grew hateful to her; she stopped its ill-omened garrulity. The twelve strokes of midnight sounded from the drawing-room.

"Ah, God!" she cried, "to see him here would be happiness. And yet, it is not so very long since he came here, brought by desire, and the tones of his voice filled this boudoir. And now there is nothing."

She remembered the times that she had played the coquette with him, and how that her coquetry had cost her her lover, and the despairing tears flowed for long.

Her woman came at length with, "Mme la Duchesse does not know, perhaps, that it is two o'clock in the morning; I thought that madame was not feeling well."

"Yes, I am going to bed," said the Duchess, drying her eyes. "But remember, Suzanne, never to come in again without orders; I tell you this for the last time."

For a week, Mme de Langeais went to every house where there was a hope of meeting M. de Montriveau. Contrary to her usual habits, she came early and went late; gave up dancing, and went to the card-tables. Her experiments were fruitless. She did not succeed in getting a glimpse of Armand. She did not dare to utter his name now. One evening, however, in a fit of despair, she spoke to Mme de Serizy, and asked as carelessly as she could, "You must have quarreled with M. de Montriveau? He is not to be seen at your house now."

The Countess laughed. "So he does not come here either?" she returned. "He is not to be seen anywhere, for that matter. He is interested in some woman, no doubt."

"I used to think that the Marquis de Ronquerolles was one of his friends——" the Duchess began sweetly.

"I have never heard my brother say that he was acquainted with him."

Mme de Langeais did not reply. Mme de Serizy concluded from the Duchess's silence that she might apply the scourge with impunity to a discreet friendship which she had seen, with bitterness of soul, for a long time past.

"So you miss that melancholy personage, do you? I have heard most extraordinary things of him. Wound his feelings, he never comes back, he forgives nothing; and, if you love him, he keeps you in chains. To everything that I said of him, one of those that praise him sky-high would always answer, 'He knows how to love!' People are always telling me that Montriveau would give up all for his friend; that his is a great nature. Pooh! society does not want such tremendous natures. Men of that stamp are all very well at home; let them stay there and leave us to our pleasant littlenesses. What do you say, Antoinette?"

Woman of the world though she was, the Duchess seemed agitated, yet she replied in a natural voice that deceived her fair friend:

"I am sorry to miss him. I took a great interest in him, and promised to myself to be his sincere friend. I like great natures, dear friend, ridiculous though you may think it. To give oneself to a fool is a clear confession, is it not, that one is governed wholly by one's senses?"

Mme de Serizy's "preferences" had always been for commonplace men; her lover at the moment, the Marquis d'Aiglemont, was a fine, tall man.

After this, the Countess soon took her departure, you may be sure Mme de Langeais saw hope in Armand's withdrawal from the world; she wrote to him at once; it was a humble, gentle letter, surely it would bring him if he loved her still. She sent her footman with it next day. On the servant's return, she asked whether he had given the letter to M. de Montriveau himself, and could not restrain the movement of joy at the affirmative answer. Armand was in Paris! He stayed alone in his house; he did not go out into society! So she was loved! All day long she waited for an answer that never came. Again and again, when impatience grew unbearable, Antoinette found reasons for his delay. Armand felt embarrassed; the reply would come by post; but night came, and she could not deceive herself any longer. It was a dreadful day, a day of pain grown sweet, of intolerable heart-throbs, a day when the heart squanders the very forces of life in riot.

Next day she sent for an answer.

"M. le Marquis sent word that he would call on Mme la Duchesse," reported Julien.

She fled lest her happiness should be seen in her face, and flung herself on her couch to devour her first sensations.

"He is coming!"

The thought rent her soul. And, in truth, woe unto those for whom suspense is not the most horrible time of tempest, while it increases and multiplies the sweetest joys; for they have nothing in them of that flame which quickens the images of things, giving to them a second existence, so that we cling as closely to the pure essence as to its outward and visible manifestation. What is suspense in love but a constant drawing upon an unfailing hope?—a submission to the terrible scourging of passion, while passion is yet happy, and the disenchantment of reality has not set in. The constant putting forth of strength and longing, called suspense, is surely, to the human soul, as fragrance to the flower that breathes it forth. We soon leave the brilliant, unsatisfying colours of tulips and coreopsis, but we turn again and again to drink in the sweetness of orange-blossoms or volkameria-flowers compared separately, each in its own land, to a betrothed bride, full of love, made fair by the past and future.

The Duchess learned the joys of this new life of hers through the rapture with which she received the scourgings of love. As this change wrought in her, she saw other destinies before her, and a better meaning in the things of life. As she hurried to her dressing-room, she understood what studied adornment and the most minute attention to her toilet mean when these are undertaken for love's sake and not for vanity. Even now this making ready helped her to bear the long time of waiting. A relapse of intense agitation set in when she was dressed; she passed through nervous paroxysms brought on by the dreadful power which sets the whole mind in ferment. Perhaps that power is only a disease, though the pain of it is sweet. The Duchess was dressed and waiting at two o'clock in the afternoon. At half-past eleven that night M. de Montriveau had not arrived. To try to give an idea of the anguish endured by a woman who might be said to be the spoilt child of civilization, would be to attempt to say how many imaginings the heart can condense into one thought. As well endeavour to measure the forces expended by the soul in a sigh whenever the bell rang; to estimate the drain of life when a carriage rolled past without stopping, and left her prostrate.

"Can he be playing with me?" she said, as the clocks struck midnight.

She grew white; her teeth chattered; she struck her hands together and leapt up and crossed the boudoir, recollecting as she did so how often he had come thither without a summons. But she resigned herself. Had she not seen him grow pale, and start up under the stinging barbs of irony? Then Mme de Langeais felt the horror of the woman's appointed lot; a man's is the active part, a woman must wait passively when she loves. If a woman goes beyond her beloved, she makes a mistake which few men can forgive; almost every man would feel that a woman lowers herself by this piece of angelic flattery. But Armand's was a great nature; he surely must be one of the very few who can repay such exceeding love by love that lasts forever.

"Well, I will make the advance," she told herself, as she tossed on her bed and found no sleep there; "I will go to him. I will not weary myself with holding out a hand to him, but I will hold it out. A man of a thousand will see a promise of love and constancy in every step that a woman takes towards him. Yes, the angels must come down from heaven to reach men; and I wish to be an angel for him."

Next day she wrote. It was a billet of the kind in which the intellects of the ten thousand Sevignes that Paris now can number particularly excel. And yet only a Duchesse de Langeais, brought up by Mme la Princesse de Blamont-Chauvry, could have written that delicious note; no other woman could complain without lowering herself; could spread wings in such a flight without draggling her pinions in humiliation; rise gracefully in revolt; scold without giving offence; and pardon without compromising her personal dignity.

Julien went with the note. Julien, like his kind, was the victim of love's marches and countermarches.

"What did M. de Montriveau reply?" she asked, as indifferently as she could, when the man came back to report himself.

"M. le Marquis requested me to tell Mme la Duchesse that it was all right."

Oh the dreadful reaction of the soul upon herself! To have her heart stretched on the rack before curious witnesses; yet not to utter a sound, to be forced to keep silence! One of the countless miseries of the rich!

More than three weeks went by. Mme de Langeais wrote again and again, and no answer came from Montriveau. At last she gave out that she was ill, to gain a dispensation from attendance on the Princess and from social duties. She was only at home to her father the Duc de Navarreins, her aunt the Princesse de Blamont-Chauvry, the old Vidame de Pamiers (her maternal great-uncle), and to her husband's uncle, the Duc de Grandlieu. These persons found no difficulty in believing that the Duchess was ill, seeing that she grew thinner and paler and more dejected every day. The vague ardour of love, the smart of wounded pride, the continual prick of the only scorn that could touch her, the yearnings towards joys that she craved with a vain continual longing—all these things told upon her, mind and body; all the forces of her nature were stimulated to no purpose. She was paying the arrears of her life of make-believe.

She went out at last to a review. M. de Montriveau was to be there. For the Duchess, on the balcony of the Tuileries with the Royal Family, it was one of those festival days that are long remembered. She looked supremely beautiful in her languor; she was greeted with admiration in all eyes. It was Montriveau's presence that made her so fair.

Once or twice they exchanged glances. The General came almost to her feet in all the glory of that soldier's uniform, which produces an effect upon the feminine imagination to which the most prudish will confess. When a woman is very much in love, and has not seen her lover for two months, such a swift moment must be something like the phase of a dream when the eyes embrace a world that stretches away forever. Only women or young men can imagine the dull, frenzied hunger in the Duchess's eyes. As for older men, if during the paroxysms of early passion in youth they had experience of such phenomena of nervous power; at a later day it is so completely forgotten that they deny the very existence of the luxuriant ecstasy— the only name that can be given to these wonderful intuitions. Religious ecstasy is the aberration of a soul that has shaken off its bonds of flesh; whereas in amorous ecstasy all the forces of soul and body are embraced and blended in one. If a woman falls a victim to the tyrannous frenzy before which Mme de Langeais was forced to bend, she will take one decisive resolution after another so swiftly that it is impossible to give account of them. Thought after thought rises and flits across her brain, as clouds are whirled by the wind across the grey veil of mist that shuts out the sun. Thenceforth the facts reveal all. And the facts are these.

The day after the review, Mme de Langeais sent her carriage and liveried servants to wait at the Marquis de Montriveau's door from eight o'clock in the morning till three in the afternoon. Armand lived in the Rue de Tournon, a few steps away from the Chamber of Peers, and that very day the House was sitting; but long before the peers returned to their palaces, several people had recognised the Duchess's carriage and liveries. The first of these was the Baron de Maulincour. That young officer had met with disdain from Mme de Langeais and a better reception from Mme de Serizy; he betook himself at once therefore to his mistress, and under seal of secrecy told her of this strange freak.

In a moment the news was spread with telegraphic speed through all the coteries in the Faubourg Saint-Germain; it reached the Tuileries and the Elysee-Bourbon; it was the sensation of the day, the matter of all the talk from noon till night. Almost everywhere the women denied the facts, but in such a manner that the report was confirmed; the men one and all believed it, and manifested a most indulgent interest in Mme de Langeais. Some among them threw the blame on Armand.

"That savage of a Montriveau is a man of bronze," said they; "he insisted on making this scandal, no doubt."

"Very well, then," others replied, "Mme de Langeais has been guilty of a most generous piece of imprudence. To renounce the world and rank, and fortune, and consideration for her lover's sake, and that in the face of all Paris, is as fine a *coup d'etat* for a woman as that barber's knife-thrust, which so affected Canning in a court of assize. Not one of the women who blame the Duchess would make a declaration worthy of ancient times. It is heroic of Mme de Langeais to proclaim herself so frankly. Now there is nothing left to her but to love Montriveau. There must be something great about a woman if she says, 'I will have but one passion.'"

"But what is to become of society, monsieur, if you honour vice in this way without respect for virtue?" asked the Comtesse de Granville, the attorney-general's wife.

While the Chateau, the Faubourg, and the Chaussee d'Antin were discussing the shipwreck of aristocratic virtue; while excited young men rushed about on horseback to make sure that the carriage was standing in the Rue de Tournon, and the Duchess in consequence was beyond a doubt in M. de Montriveau's rooms, Mme de Langeais, with heavy throbbing pulses, was lying hidden away in her boudoir. And Armand?—he had been out all night, and at that moment was walking with M. de Marsay in the Gardens of the Tuileries. The elder members, of Mme de Langeais' family were engaged in calling upon one another, arranging to read her a homily and to hold a consultation as to the best way of putting a stop to the scandal.

At three o'clock, therefore, M. le Duc de Navarreins, the Vidame de Pamiers, the old Princesse de Blamont-Chauvry, and the Duc de Grandlieu were assembled in Mme la Duchesse de Langeais' drawing-room. To them, as to all curious inquirers, the servants said that their mistress was not at home; the Duchess had made no exceptions to her orders. But these four personages shone conspicuous in that lofty sphere, of which the revolutions and hereditary pretensions are solemnly recorded year by year in the *Almanach de Gotha*, wherefore without some slight sketch of each of them this picture of society were incomplete.

The Princesse de Blamont-Chauvry, in the feminine world, was a most poetic wreck of the reign of Louis Quinze. In her beautiful prime, so it was said, she had done her part to win for that monarch his appellation of *le Bien-aime*. Of her past charms of feature, little remained save a remarkably prominent slender nose, curved like a Turkish scimitar, now the principal ornament of a countenance that put you in mind of an old white glove. Add a few powdered curls, high-heeled pantoufles, a cap with upstanding loops of lace, black mittens, and a decided taste for *ombre*. But to do full justice to the lady, it must be said that she appeared in low-necked gowns of an evening (so high an opinion of her ruins had she), wore long gloves, and raddled her cheeks with Martin's classic rouge. An appalling amiability in her wrinkles, a prodigious brightness in the old lady's eyes, a profound dignity in her whole person, together with the triple barbed wit of her tongue, and an infallible memory in her head, made of her a real power in the land. The whole Cabinet des Chartes was entered in duplicate on the parchment of her brain. She knew all the genealogies of every noble house in Europe—princes, dukes, and counts—and could put her hand on the last descendants of Charlemagne in the direct line. No usurpation of title could escape the Princesse de Blamont-Chauvry.

110

Young men who wished to stand well at Court, ambitious men, and young married women paid her assiduous homage. Her salon set the tone of the Faubourg Saint-Germain. The words of this Talleyrand in petticoats were taken as final decrees. People came to consult her on questions of etiquette or usages, or to take lessons in good taste. And, in truth, no other old woman could put back her snuff-box in her pocket as the Princess could; while there was a precision and a grace about the movements of her skirts, when she sat down or crossed her feet, which drove the finest ladies of the young generation to despair. Her voice had remained in her head during one-third of her lifetime; but she could not prevent a descent into the membranes of the nose, which lent to it a peculiar expressiveness. She still retained a hundred and fifty thousand livres of her great fortune, for Napoleon had generously returned her woods to her; so that personally and in the matter of possessions she was a woman of no little consequence.

This curious antique, seated in a low chair by the fireside, was chatting with the Vidame de Pamiers, a contemporary ruin. The Vidame was a big, tall, and spare man, a seigneur of the old school, and had been a Commander of the Order of Malta. His neck had always been so tightly compressed by a strangulation stock, that his cheeks pouched over it a little, and he held his head high; to many people this would have given an air of self-sufficiency, but in the Vidame it was justified by a Voltairean wit. His wide prominent eyes seemed to see everything, and as a matter of fact there was not much that they had not seen. Altogether, his person was a perfect model of aristocratic outline, slim and slender, supple and agreeable. He seemed as if he could be pliant or rigid at will, and twist and bend, or rear his head like a snake.

The Duc de Navarreins was pacing up and down the room with the Duc de Grandlieu. Both were men of fifty-six or thereabouts, and still hale; both were short, corpulent, flourishing, somewhat florid-complexioned men with jaded eyes, and lower lips that had begun to hang already. But for an exquisite refinement of accent, an urbane courtesy, and an ease of manner that could change in a moment to insolence, a superficial observer might have taken them for a couple of bankers. Any such mistake would have been impossible, however, if the listener could have heard them converse, and seen them on their guard with men whom they feared, vapid and commonplace with their equals, slippery with the inferiors whom courtiers and statesmen know how to tame by a tactful word, or to humiliate with an unexpected phrase.

Such were the representatives of the great noblesse that determined to perish rather than submit to any change. It was a noblesse that deserved praise and blame in equal measure; a noblesse that will never be judged impartially until some poet shall arise to tell how joyfully the nobles obeyed the King though their heads fell under a Richelieu's axe, and how deeply they scorned the guillotine of '89 as a foul revenge.

Another noticeable trait in all the four was a thin voice that agreed peculiarly well with their ideas and bearing. Among themselves, at any rate, they were on terms of perfect equality. None of them betrayed any sign of annoyance over the Duchess's escapade, but all of them had learned at Court to hide their feelings.

And here, lest critics should condemn the puerility of the opening of the forthcoming scene, it is perhaps as well to remind the reader that Locke, once happening to be in the company of several great lords, renowned no less for their wit than for their breeding and political consistency, wickedly amused himself by taking down their conversation by some shorthand process of his own; and afterwards, when he read it over to them to see what they could make of it, they all burst out laughing. And, in truth, the tinsel jargon which circulates among the upper ranks in every country yields mighty little gold to the crucible when washed in the ashes of literature or philosophy. In every rank of society (some few Parisian salons excepted) the curious observer finds folly a constant quantity beneath a more or less transparent varnish. Conversation with any substance in it is a rare exception, and boeotianism is current coin in every zone. In the higher regions they must perforce talk more, but to make up for it they think the less. Thinking is a tiring exercise, and the rich like their lives to flow by easily and without effort. It is by comparing the fundamental matter of jests, as you rise in the social scale from the street-boy to the peer of France, that the observer arrives at a true comprehension of M. de Talleyrand's maxim, "The manner is everything"; an elegant rendering of the legal axiom, "The form is of more consequence than the matter." In the eyes of the poet the advantage rests with the lower classes, for they seldom fail to give a certain character of rude poetry to their thoughts. Perhaps also this same observation may explain the sterility of the salons, their emptiness, their shallowness, and the repugnance felt by men of ability for bartering their ideas for such pitiful small change.

The Duke suddenly stopped as if some bright idea occurred to him, and remarked to his neighbour:

"So you have sold Tornthon?"

"No, he is ill. I am very much afraid I shall lose him, and I should be uncommonly sorry. He is a very good hunter. Do you know how the Duchesse de Marigny is?"

"No. I did not go this morning. I was just going out to call when you came in to speak about Antoinette. But yesterday she was very ill indeed; they had given her up, she took the sacrament."

"Her death will make a change in your cousin's position."

"Not at all. She gave away her property in her lifetime, only keeping an annuity. She made over the Guebriant estate to her niece, Mme de Soulanges, subject to a yearly charge."

"It will be a great loss for society. She was a kind woman. Her family will miss her; her experience and advice carried weight. Her son Marigny is an amiable man; he has a sharp wit, he can talk. He is pleasant, very pleasant. Pleasant? oh, that no one can deny, but—ill regulated to the last degree. Well, and yet it is an extraordinary thing, he is very acute. He was dining at the club the other day with that moneyed Chaussee-d'Antin set. Your uncle (he always goes there for his game of cards) found him there to his astonishment, and asked if he was a member. 'Yes,' said he, 'I don't go into society now; I am living among the bankers.'—You know why?" added the Marquis, with a meaning smile.

"No," said the Duke.

"He is smitten with that little Mme Keller, Gondreville's daughter; she is only lately married, and has a great vogue, they say, in that set."

"Well, Antoinette does not find time heavy on her hands, it seems," remarked the Vidame.

"My affection for that little woman has driven me to find a singular pastime," replied the Princess, as she returned her snuff-box to her pocket.

"Dear aunt, I am extremely vexed," said the Duke, stopping short in his walk. "Nobody but one of Bonaparte's men could ask such an indecorous thing of a woman of fashion. Between ourselves, Antoinette might have made a better choice."

"The Montriveaus are a very old family and very well connected, my dear," replied the Princess; "they are related to all the noblest houses of Burgundy. If the Dulmen branch of the Arschoot Rivaudoults should come to an end in Galicia, the Montriveaus would succeed to the Arschoot title and estates. They inherit through their great-grandfather.

"Are you sure?"

"I know it better than this Montriveau's father did. I told him about it, I used to see a good deal of him; and, Chevalier of several orders though he was, he only laughed; he was an encyclopaedist. But his brother turned the relationship to good account during the emigration. I have heard it said that his northern kinsfolk were most kind in every way — —"

"Yes, to be sure. The Comte de Montriveau died at St. Petersburg," said the Vidame. "I met him there. He was a big man with an incredible passion for oysters."

"However many did he eat?" asked the Duc de Grandlieu.

"Ten dozen every day."

"And did they not disagree with him?"

"Not the least bit in the world."

"Why, that is extraordinary! Had he neither the stone nor gout, nor any other complaint, in consequence?"

"No; his health was perfectly good, and he died through an accident."

"By accident! Nature prompted him to eat oysters, so probably he required them; for up to a certain point our predominant tastes are conditions of our existence."

"I am of your opinion," said the Princess, with a smile.

"Madame, you always put a malicious construction on things," returned the Marquis.

"I only want you to understand that these remarks might leave a wrong impression on a young woman's mind," said she, and interrupted herself to exclaim, "But this niece, this niece of mine!"

"Dear aunt, I still refuse to believe that she can have gone to M. de Montriveau," said the Duc de Navarreins.

"Bah!" returned the Princess.

"What do you think, Vidame?" asked the Marquis.

"If the Duchess were an artless simpleton, I should think that ——"

"But when a woman is in love she becomes an artless simpleton," retorted the Princess. "Really, my poor Vidame, you must be getting older."

"After all, what is to be done?" asked the Duke.

"If my dear niece is wise," said the Princess, "she will go to Court this evening — fortunately, today is Monday, and reception day — and you must see that we all rally round her and give the lie to this absurd rumour. There are hundreds of ways of explaining things; and if the Marquis de Montriveau is a gentleman, he will come to our assistance. We will bring these children to listen to reason ——"

"But, dear aunt, it is not easy to tell M. de Montriveau the truth to his face. He is one of Bonaparte's pupils, and he has a position. Why, he is one of the great men of the day; he is high up in the Guards, and very useful there. He has not a spark of ambition. He is just the man to say, 'Here is my commission, leave me in peace,' if the King should say a word that he did not like."

"Then, pray, what are his opinions?"

"Very unsound."

"Really," sighed the Princess, "the King is, as he always has been, a Jacobin under the Lilies of France."

"Oh! not quite so bad," said the Vidame.

"Yes; I have known him for a long while. The man that pointed out the Court to his wife on the occasion of her first state dinner in public with, 'These are our people,' could only be a black-hearted scoundrel. I can see Monsieur exactly the same as ever in the King. The bad brother who voted so wrongly in his department of the Constituent Assembly was sure to compound with the Liberals and allow them to argue and talk. This philosophical cant will be just as dangerous now for the younger brother as it used to be for the elder; this fat man with the little mind is amusing himself by creating difficulties, and how his successor is to get out of them I do not know; he holds his younger brother in abhorrence; he would be glad to think as he lay dying, 'He will not reign very long — —'"

"Aunt, he is the King, and I have the honour to be in his service — —"

"But does your post take away your right of free speech, my dear? You come of quite as good a house as the Bourbons. If the Guises had shown a little more resolution, His Majesty would be a nobody at this day. It is time I went out of this world, the noblesse is dead. Yes, it is all over with you, my children," she continued, looking as she spoke at the Vidame. "What has my niece done that the whole town should be talking about her? She is in the wrong; I disapprove of her conduct, a useless scandal is a blunder; that is why I still have my doubts about this want of regard for appearances; I brought her up, and I know that — —"

Just at that moment the Duchess came out of her boudoir. She had recognised her aunt's voice and heard the name of Montriveau. She was still in her loose morning-gown; and even as she came in, M. de Grandlieu, looking carelessly out of the window, saw his niece's carriage driving back along the street. The Duke took his daughter's face in both hands and kissed her on the forehead.

"So, dear girl," he said, "you do not know what is going on?"

"Has anything extraordinary happened, father dear?"

"Why, all Paris believes that you are with M. de Montriveau."

"My dear Antoinette, you were at home all the time, were you not?" said the Princess, holding out a hand, which the Duchess kissed with affectionate respect.

"Yes, dear mother; I was at home all the time. And," she added, as she turned to greet the Vidame and the Marquis, "I wished that all Paris should think that I was with M. de Montriveau."

The Duke flung up his hands, struck them together in despair, and folded his arms.

"Then, cannot you see what will come of this mad freak?" he asked at last.

But the aged Princess had suddenly risen, and stood looking steadily at the Duchess, the younger woman flushed, and her eyes fell. Mme de Chauvry gently drew her closer, and said, "My little angel, let me kiss you!"

She kissed her niece very affectionately on the forehead, and continued smiling, while she held her hand in a tight clasp.

"We are not under the Valois now, dear child. You have compromised your husband and your position. Still, we will arrange to make everything right."

"But, dear aunt, I do not wish to make it right at all. It is my wish that all Paris should say that I was with M. de Montriveau this morning. If you destroy that belief, however ill grounded it may be, you will do me a singular disservice."

"Do you really wish to ruin yourself, child, and to grieve your family?"

"My family, father, unintentionally condemned me to irreparable misfortune when they sacrificed me to family considerations. You

117

may, perhaps, blame me for seeking alleviations, but you will certainly feel for me."

"After all the endless pains you take to settle your daughters suitably!" muttered M. de Navarreins, addressing the Vidame.

The Princess shook a stray grain of snuff from her skirts. "My dear little girl," she said, "be happy, if you can. We are not talking of troubling your felicity, but of reconciling it with social usages. We all of us here assembled know that marriage is a defective institution tempered by love. But when you take a lover, is there any need to make your bed in the Place du Carrousel? See now, just be a bit reasonable, and hear what we have to say."

"I am listening."

"Mme la Duchesse," began the Duc de Grandlieu, "if it were any part of an uncle's duty to look after his nieces, he ought to have a position; society would owe him honours and rewards and a salary, exactly as if he were in the King's service. So I am not here to talk about my nephew, but of your own interests. Let us look ahead a little. If you persist in making a scandal—I have seen the animal before, and I own that I have no great liking for him—Langeais is stingy enough, and he does not care a rap for anyone but himself; he will have a separation; he will stick to your money, and leave you poor, and consequently you will be a nobody. The income of a hundred thousand livres that you have just inherited from your maternal great-aunt will go to pay for his mistresses' amusements. You will be bound and gagged by the law; you will have to say *Amen* to all these arrangements. Suppose M. de Montriveau leaves you——dear me! do not let us put ourselves in a passion, my dear niece; a man does not leave a woman while she is young and pretty; still, we have seen so many pretty women left disconsolate, even among princesses, that you will permit the supposition, an all but impossible supposition I quite wish to believe.——Well, suppose that he goes, what will become of you without a husband? Keep well with your husband as you take care of your beauty; for beauty, after all, is a woman's parachute, and a husband also stands between you and worse. I am supposing that you are happy and loved to the end, and I am leaving unpleasant or unfortunate events altogether out of the reckoning. This being so, fortunately or unfortunately, you may have children. What are they to be? Montriveaus? Very well; they certainly will not succeed to their father's whole fortune. You will want to give them all that you have; he will wish to do the same. Nothing more natural, dear me! And you will find the law against you. How many times have we seen heirs-at-law bringing a law-suit to recover the property from illegitimate children? Every court of law rings with such actions all over the world. You will create a *fidei commissum* perhaps; and if the trustee betrays your confidence, your children have no remedy against him; and they are ruined. So choose carefully. You see the perplexities of the position. In every possible way your children will be sacrificed of necessity to the fancies of your heart; they will have no recognised status. While they are little they will be charming; but, Lord! some day they will reproach you for thinking of no one but your two selves. We old gentlemen know all about it. Little boys grow up into men, and men are ungrateful beings. When I was in Germany, did I not hear young de Horn say, after supper, 'If my mother had been an honest woman, I should be prince-regnant!' *If?'* We have spent our lives in hearing plebeians say *if*. *If* brought about the Revolution. When a man cannot lay the blame on his father or mother, he holds God responsible for his hard lot. In short, dear child, we are here to open your eyes. I will say all I have to say in a few words, on which you had better meditate: A woman ought never to put her husband in the right."

"Uncle, so long as I cared for nobody, I could calculate; I looked at interests then, as you do; now, I can only feel."

"But, my dear little girl," remonstrated the Vidame, "life is simply a complication of interests and feelings; to be happy, more particularly in your position, one must try to reconcile one's feelings with one's interests. A grisette may love according to her fancy, that is intelligible enough, but you have a pretty fortune, a family, a name and a place at Court, and you ought not to fling them out of the window. And what have we been asking you to do to keep them all?—To manoeuvre carefully instead of falling foul of social conventions. Lord! I shall very soon be eighty years old, and I cannot recollect, under any regime, a love worth the price that you are willing to pay for the love of this lucky young man."

119

The Duchess silenced the Vidame with a look; if Montriveau could have seen that glance, he would have forgiven all.

"It would be very effective on the stage," remarked the Duc de Grandlieu, "but it all amounts to nothing when your jointure and position and independence is concerned. You are not grateful, my dear niece. You will not find many families where the relatives have courage enough to teach the wisdom gained by experience, and to make rash young heads listen to reason. Renounce your salvation in two minutes, if it pleases you to damn yourself; well and good; but reflect well beforehand when it comes to renouncing your income. I know of no confessor who remits the pains of poverty. I have a right, I think, to speak in this way to you; for if you are ruined, I am the one person who can offer you a refuge. I am almost an uncle to Langeais, and I alone have a right to put him in the wrong."

The Duc de Navarreins roused himself from painful reflections.

"Since you speak of feeling, my child," he said, "let me remind you that a woman who bears your name ought to be moved by sentiments which do not touch ordinary people. Can you wish to give an advantage to the Liberals, to those Jesuits of Robespierre's that are doing all they can to vilify the noblesse? Some things a Navarreins cannot do without failing in duty to his house. You would not be alone in your dishonor — —"

"Come, come!" said the Princess. "Dishonor? Do not make such a fuss about the journey of an empty carriage, children, and leave me alone with Antoinette. All three of you come and dine with me. I will undertake to arrange matters suitably. You men understand nothing; you are beginning to talk sourly already, and I have no wish to see a quarrel between you and my dear child. Do me the pleasure to go."

The three gentlemen probably guessed the Princess's intentions; they took their leave. M. de Navarreins kissed his daughter on the forehead with, "Come, be good, dear child. It is not too late yet if you choose."

"Couldn't we find some good fellow in the family to pick a quarrel with this Montriveau?" said the Vidame, as they went downstairs.

When the two women were alone, the Princess beckoned her niece to a little low chair by her side.

"My pearl," said she, "in this world below, I know nothing worse calumniated than God and the eighteenth century; for as I look back over my own young days, I do not recollect that a single duchess trampled the proprieties underfoot as you have just done. Novelists and scribblers brought the reign of Louis XV into disrepute. Do not believe them. The du Barry, my dear, was quite as good as the Widow Scarron, and the more agreeable woman of the two. In my time a woman could keep her dignity among her gallantries. Indiscretion was the ruin of us, and the beginning of all the mischief. The philosophists—the nobodies whom we admitted into our salons—had no more gratitude or sense of decency than to make an inventory of our hearts, to traduce us one and all, and to rail against the age by way of a return for our kindness. The people are not in a position to judge of anything whatsoever; they looked at the facts, not at the form. But the men and women of those times, my heart, were quite as remarkable as at any other period of the Monarchy. Not one of your Werthers, none of your notabilities, as they are called, never a one of your men in yellow kid gloves and trousers that disguise the poverty of their legs, would cross Europe in the dress of a travelling hawker to brave the daggers of a Duke of Modena, and to shut himself up in the dressing-room of the Regent's daughter at the risk of his life. Not one of your little consumptive patients with their tortoiseshell eyeglasses would hide himself in a closet for six weeks, like Lauzun, to keep up his mistress's courage while she was lying in of her child. There was more passion in M. de Jaucourt's little finger than in your whole race of higglers that leave a woman to better themselves elsewhere! Just tell me where to find the page that would be cut in pieces and buried under the floorboards for one kiss on the Konigsmark's gloved finger!

"Really, it would seem today that the roles are exchanged, and women are expected to show their devotion for men. These modern gentlemen are worth less, and think more of themselves. Believe me, my dear, all these adventures that have been made public, and now are turned against our good Louis XV, were kept quite secret at first. If it had not been for a pack of poetasters, scribblers, and moralists, who hung about our waiting-women, and took down their slanders, our epoch would have appeared in literature as a well-conducted age. I am justifying the century and not its fringe. Perhaps a hundred women of quality were lost; but for every one, the rogues set down ten, like the gazettes after a battle when they count up the losses of the beaten side. And in any case I do not know that the Revolution and the Empire can reproach us; they were coarse, dull, licentious times. Faugh! it is revolting. Those are the brothels of French history.

"This preamble, my dear child," she continued after a pause, "brings me to the thing that I have to say. If you care for Montriveau, you are quite at liberty to love him at your ease, and as much as you can. I know by experience that, unless you are locked up (but locking people up is out of fashion now), you will do as you please; I should have done the same at your age. Only, sweetheart, I should not have given up my right to be the mother of future Ducs de Langeais. So mind appearances. The Vidame is right. No man is worth a single one of the sacrifices which we are foolish enough to make for their love. Put yourself in such a position that you may still be M. de Langeais' wife, in case you should have the misfortune to repent. When you are an old woman, you will be very glad to hear mass said at Court, and not in some provincial convent. Therein lies the whole question. A single imprudence means an allowance and a wandering life; it means that you are at the mercy of your lover; it means that you must put up with insolence from women that are not so honest, precisely because they have been very vulgarly sharp-witted. It would be a hundred times better to go to Montriveau's at night in a cab, and disguised, instead of sending your carriage in broad daylight. You are a little fool, my dear child! Your carriage flattered his vanity; your person would have ensnared his heart. All this that I have said is just and true; but, for my own part, I do not blame you. You are two centuries behind the times with your false ideas of greatness. There, leave us to arrange your affairs, and say that Montriveau made your servants drunk to gratify his vanity and to compromise you——"

The Duchess rose to her feet with a spring. "In Heaven's name, aunt, do not slander him!"

The old Princess's eyes flashed.

"Dear child," she said, "I should have liked to spare such of your illusions as were not fatal. But there must be an end of all illusions now. You would soften me if I were not so old. Come, now, do not vex him, or us, or anyone else. I will undertake to satisfy everybody; but promise me not to permit yourself a single step henceforth until you have consulted me. Tell me all, and perhaps I may bring it all right again."

"Aunt, I promise ——"

"To tell me everything?"

"Yes, everything. Everything that can be told."

"But, my sweetheart, it is precisely what cannot be told that I want to know. Let us understand each other thoroughly. Come, let me put my withered old lips on your beautiful forehead. No; let me do as I wish. I forbid you to kiss my bones. Old people have a courtesy of their own.... There, take me down to my carriage," she added, when she had kissed her niece.

"Then may I go to him in disguise, dear aunt?"

"Why — yes. The story can always be denied," said the old Princess.

This was the one idea which the Duchess had clearly grasped in the sermon. When Mme de Chauvry was seated in the corner of her carriage, Mme de Langeais bade her a graceful adieu and went up to her room. She was quite happy again.

"My person would have snared his heart; my aunt is right; a man cannot surely refuse a pretty woman when she understands how to offer herself."

That evening, at the Elysee-Bourbon, the Duc de Navarreins, M. de Pamiers, M. de Marsay, M. de Grandlieu, and the Duc de Maufrigneuse triumphantly refuted the scandals that were circulating with regard to the Duchesse de Langeais. So many officers and other persons had seen Montriveau walking in the Tuileries that morning, that the silly story was set down to chance, which takes all that is offered. And so, in spite of the fact that the Duchess's carriage had waited before Montriveau's door, her

123

character became as clear and as spotless as Membrino's sword after Sancho had polished it up.

But, at two o'clock, M. de Ronquerolles passed Montriveau in a deserted alley, and said with a smile, "She is coming on, is your Duchess. Go on, keep it up!" he added, and gave a significant cut of the riding whip to his mare, who sped off like a bullet down the avenue.

Two days after the fruitless scandal, Mme de Langeais wrote to M. de Montriveau. That letter, like the preceding ones, remained unanswered. This time she took her own measures, and bribed M. de Montriveau's man, Auguste. And so at eight o'clock that evening she was introduced into Armand's apartment. It was not the room in which that secret scene had passed; it was entirely different. The Duchess was told that the General would not be at home that night. Had he two houses? The man would give no answer. Mme de Langeais had bought the key of the room, but not the man's whole loyalty.

When she was left alone she saw her fourteen letters lying on an old-fashioned stand, all of them uncreased and unopened. He had not read them. She sank into an easy-chair, and for a while she lost consciousness. When she came to herself, Auguste was holding vinegar for her to inhale.

"A carriage; quick!" she ordered.

The carriage came. She hastened downstairs with convulsive speed, and left orders that no one was to be admitted. For twenty-four hours she lay in bed, and would have no one near her but her woman, who brought her a cup of orange-flower water from time to time. Suzette heard her mistress moan once or twice, and caught a glimpse of tears in the brilliant eyes, now circled with dark shadows.

The next day, amid despairing tears, Mme de Langeais took her resolution. Her man of business came for an interview, and no doubt received instructions of some kind. Afterwards she sent for the Vidame de Pamiers; and while she waited, she wrote a letter to M. de Montriveau. The Vidame punctually came towards two o'clock that afternoon, to find his young cousin looking white and worn, but resigned; never had her divine loveliness been more poetic than now in the languor of her agony.

"You owe this assignation to your eighty-four years, dear cousin," she said. "Ah! do not smile, I beg of you, when an unhappy woman has reached the lowest depths of wretchedness. You are a gentleman, and after the adventures of your youth you must feel some indulgence for women."

"None whatever," said he.

"Indeed!"

"Everything is in their favour."

"Ah! Well, you are one of the inner family circle; possibly you will be the last relative, the last friend whose hand I shall press, so I can ask your good offices. Will you, dear Vidame, do me a service which I could not ask of my own father, nor of my uncle Grandlieu, nor of any woman? You cannot fail to understand. I beg of you to do my bidding, and then to forget what you have done, whatever may come of it. It is this: Will you take this letter and go to M. de Montriveau? will you see him yourself, give it into his hands, and ask him, as you men can ask things between yourselves—for you have a code of honour between man and man which you do not use with us, and a different way of regarding things between yourselves—ask him if he will read this letter? Not in your presence. Certain feelings men hide from each other. I give you authority to say, if you think it necessary to bring him, that it is a question of life or death for me. If he deigns — —"

"*Deigns!*" repeated the Vidame.

"If he deigns to read it," the Duchess continued with dignity, "say one thing more. You will go to see him about five o'clock, for I know that he will dine at home today at that time. Very good. By way of answer he must come to see me. If, three hours afterwards, by eight o'clock, he does not leave his house, all will be over. The Duchesse de Langeais will have vanished from the world. I shall not be dead, dear friend, no, but no human power will ever find me again on this earth. Come and dine with me; I shall at least have one friend with me in the last agony. Yes, dear cousin, tonight will decide my fate;

and whatever happens to me, I pass through an ordeal by fire. There! not a word. I will hear nothing of the nature of comment or advice——Let us chat and laugh together," she added, holding out a hand, which he kissed. "We will be like two grey-headed philosophers who have learned how to enjoy life to the last moment. I will look my best; I will be very enchanting for you. You perhaps will be the last man to set eyes on the Duchesse de Langeais."

The Vicomte bowed, took the letter, and went without a word. At five o'clock he returned. His cousin had studied to please him, and she looked lovely indeed. The room was gay with flowers as if for a festivity; the dinner was exquisite. For the grey-headed Vidame the Duchess displayed all the brilliancy of her wit; she was more charming than she had ever been before. At first the Vidame tried to look on all these preparations as a young woman's jest; but now and again the attempted illusion faded, the spell of his fair cousin's charm was broken. He detected a shudder caused by some kind of sudden dread, and once she seemed to listen during a pause.

"What is the matter?" he asked.

"Hush!" she said.

At seven o'clock the Duchess left him for a few minutes. When she came back again she was dressed as her maid might have dressed for a journey. She asked her guest to be her escort, took his arm, sprang into a hackney coach, and by a quarter to eight they stood outside M. de Montriveau's door.

Armand meantime had been reading the following letter:—

"MY FRIEND,—I went to your rooms for a few minutes without your knowledge; I found my letters there, and took them away. This cannot be indifference, Armand, between us; and hatred would show itself quite differently. If you love me, make an end of this cruel play, or you will kill me, and afterwards, learning how much you were loved, you might be in despair. If I have not rightly understood you, if you have no feeling towards me but aversion, which implies both contempt and disgust, then I give up all hope. A man never recovers from those feelings. You will have no regrets. Dreadful though that thought may be, it will comfort me in my long sorrow. Regrets? Oh, my Armand, may I never know of them; if I thought that I had caused you a single regret— —But, no, I will not tell you what desolation I should feel. I should be living still, and I could not be your wife; it would be too late!

"Now that I have given myself wholly to you in thought, to whom else should I give myself?—to God. The eyes that you loved for a little while shall never look on another man's face; and may the glory of God blind them to all besides. I shall never hear human voices more since I heard yours—so gentle at the first, so terrible yesterday; for it seems to me that I am still only on the morrow of your vengeance. And now may the will of God consume me. Between His wrath and yours, my friend, there will be nothing left for me but a little space for tears and prayers.

"Perhaps you wonder why I write to you? Ah! do not think ill of me if I keep a gleam of hope, and give one last sigh to happy life before I take leave of it forever. I am in a hideous position. I feel all the inward serenity that comes when a great resolution has been taken, even while I hear the last growlings of the storm. When you went out on that terrible adventure which so drew me to you, Armand, you went from the desert to the oasis with a good guide to show you the way. Well, I am going out of the oasis into the desert, and you are a pitiless guide to me. And yet you only, my friend, can understand how melancholy it is to look back for the last time on happiness—to you, and you only, I can make moan without a blush. If you grant my entreaty, I shall be happy; if you are inexorable, I shall expiate the wrong that I have done. After all, it is natural, is it not, that a woman should wish to live, invested with all noble feelings, in her friend's memory? Oh! my one and only love, let her to whom you gave life go down into the tomb in the belief that she is great in your eyes. Your harshness led me to reflect; and now that I love you so, it seems to me that I am less guilty than you think. Listen to my justification, I owe it to you; and you that are all the world to me, owe me at least a moment's justice.

"I have learned by my own anguish all that I made you suffer by my coquetry; but in those days I was utterly ignorant of love. *You* know what the torture is, and you mete it out to me! During those first eight months that you gave me you never roused any feeling of love in me. Do you ask why this was so, my friend? I can no more explain

127

it than I can tell you why I love you now. Oh! certainly it flattered my vanity that I should be the subject of your passionate talk, and receive those burning glances of yours; but you left me cold. No, I was not a woman; I had no conception of womanly devotion and happiness. Who was to blame? You would have despised me, would you not, if I had given myself without the impulse of passion? Perhaps it is the highest height to which we can rise—to give all and receive no joy; perhaps there is no merit in yielding oneself to bliss that is foreseen and ardently desired. Alas, my friend, I can say this now; these thoughts came to me when I played with you; and you seemed to me so great even then that I would not have you owe the gift to pity——What is this that I have written?

"I have taken back all my letters; I am flinging them one by one on the fire; they are burning. You will never know what they confessed—all the love and the passion and the madness——

"I will say no more, Armand; I will stop. I will not say another word of my feelings. If my prayers have not echoed from my soul through yours, I also, woman that I am, decline to owe your love to your pity. It is my wish to be loved, because you cannot choose but love me, or else to be left without mercy. If you refuse to read this letter, it shall be burnt. If, after you have read it, you do not come to me within three hours, to be henceforth forever my husband, the one man in the world for me; then I shall never blush to know that this letter is in your hands, the pride of my despair will protect my memory from all insult, and my end shall be worthy of my love. When you see me no more on earth, albeit I shall still be alive, you yourself will not think without a shudder of the woman who, in three hours' time, will live only to overwhelm you with her tenderness; a woman consumed by a hopeless love, and faithful—not to memories of past joys—but to a love that was slighted.

"The Duchesse de la Valliere wept for lost happiness and vanished power; but the Duchesse de Langeais will be happy that she may weep and be a power for you still. Yes, you will regret me. I see clearly that I was not of this world, and I thank you for making it clear to me.

"Farewell; you will never touch *my* axe. Yours was the executioner's axe, mine is God's; yours kills, mine saves. Your love was but mortal, it could not endure disdain or ridicule; mine can endure all things without growing weaker, it will last eternally. Ah! I feel a sombre joy in crushing you that believe yourself so great; in humbling you with the calm, indulgent smile of one of the least among the angels that lie at the feet of God, for to them is given the right and the power to protect and watch over men in His name. You have but felt fleeting desires, while the poor nun will shed the light of her ceaseless and ardent prayer about you, she will shelter you all your life long beneath the wings of a love that has nothing of earth in it.

"I have a presentiment of your answer; our trysting place shall be— in heaven. Strength and weakness can both enter there, dear Armand; the strong and the weak are bound to suffer. This thought soothes the anguish of my final ordeal. So calm am I that I should fear that I had ceased to love you if I were not about to leave the world for your sake.

"ANTOINETTE."

"Dear Vidame," said the Duchess as they reached Montriveau's house, "do me the kindness to ask at the door whether he is at home." The Vidame, obedient after the manner of the eighteenth century to a woman's wish, got out, and came back to bring his cousin an affirmative answer that sent a shudder through her. She grasped his hand tightly in hers, suffered him to kiss her on either cheek, and begged him to go at once. He must not watch her movements nor try to protect her. "But the people passing in the street," he objected.

"No one can fail in respect to me," she said. It was the last word spoken by the Duchess and the woman of fashion.

The Vidame went. Mme de Langeais wrapped herself about in her cloak, and stood on the doorstep until the clocks struck eight. The last stroke died away. The unhappy woman waited ten, fifteen minutes; to the last she tried to see a fresh humiliation in the delay, then her faith ebbed. She turned to leave the fatal threshold.

"Oh, God!" the cry broke from her in spite of herself; it was the first word spoken by the Carmelite.

Montriveau and some of his friends were talking together. He tried to hasten them to a conclusion, but his clock was slow, and by the time he started out for the Hotel de Langeais the Duchess was hurrying on foot through the streets of Paris, goaded by the dull rage in her heart. She reached the Boulevard d'Enfer, and looked out for the last time through falling tears on the noisy, smoky city that lay below in a red mist, lighted up by its own lamps. Then she hailed a cab, and drove away, never to return. When the Marquis de Montriveau reached the Hotel de Langeais, and found no trace of his mistress, he thought that he had been duped. He hurried away at once to the Vidame, and found that worthy gentleman in the act of slipping on his flowered dressing-gown, thinking the while of his fair cousin's happiness.

Montriveau gave him one of the terrific glances that produced the effect of an electric shock on men and women alike.

"Is it possible that you have lent yourself to some cruel hoax, monsieur?" Montriveau exclaimed. "I have just come from Mme de Langeais' house; the servants say that she is out."

"Then a great misfortune has happened, no doubt," returned the Vidame, "and through your fault. I left the Duchess at your door — —"

"When?"

"At a quarter to eight."

"Good evening," returned Montriveau, and he hurried home to ask the porter whether he had seen a lady standing on the doorstep that evening.

"Yes, my Lord Marquis, a handsome woman, who seemed very much put out. She was crying like a Magdalen, but she never made a sound, and stood as upright as a post. Then at last she went, and my wife and I that were watching her while she could not see us, heard her say, 'Oh, God!' so that it went to our hearts, asking your pardon, to hear her say it."

Montriveau, in spite of all his firmness, turned pale at those few words. He wrote a few lines to Ronquerolles, sent off the message at once, and went up to his rooms. Ronquerolles came just about midnight.

Armand gave him the Duchess's letter to read.

"Well?" asked Ronquerolles.

"She was here at my door at eight o'clock; at a quarter-past eight she had gone. I have lost her, and I love her. Oh! if my life were my own, I could blow my brains out."

"Pooh, pooh! Keep cool," said Ronquerolles. "Duchesses do not fly off like wagtails. She cannot travel faster than three leagues an hour, and tomorrow we will ride six.—Confound it! Mme de Langeais is no ordinary woman," he continued. "Tomorrow we will all of us mount and ride. The police will put us on her track during the day. She must have a carriage; angels of that sort have no wings. We shall find her whether she is on the road or hidden in Paris. There is the semaphore. We can stop her. You shall be happy. But, my dear fellow, you have made a blunder, of which men of your energy are very often guilty. They judge others by themselves, and do not know the point when human nature gives way if you strain the cords too tightly. Why did you not say a word to me sooner? I would have told you to be punctual. Good-bye till tomorrow," he added, as Montriveau said nothing. "Sleep if you can," he added, with a grasp of the hand.

But the greatest resources which society has ever placed at the disposal of statesmen, kings, ministers, bankers, or any human power, in fact, were all exhausted in vain. Neither Montriveau nor his friends could find any trace of the Duchess. It was clear that she had entered a convent. Montriveau determined to search, or to institute a search, for her through every convent in the world. He must have her, even at the cost of all the lives in a town. And in justice to this extraordinary man, it must be said that his frenzied passion awoke to the same ardour daily and lasted through five years. Only in 1829 did the Duc de Navarreins hear by chance that his daughter had travelled to Spain as Lady Julia Hopwood's maid, that she had left her service at Cadiz, and that Lady Julia never discovered that Mlle Caroline was the illustrious duchess whose sudden disappearance filled the minds of the highest society of Paris.

The feelings of the two lovers when they met again on either side of the grating in the Carmelite convent should now be comprehended to the full, and the violence of the passion awakened in either soul will doubtless explain the catastrophe of the story.

In 1823 the Duc de Langeais was dead, and his wife was free. Antoinette de Navarreins was living, consumed by love, on a ledge of rock in the Mediterranean; but it was in the Pope's power to dissolve Sister Theresa's vows. The happiness bought by so much love might yet bloom for the two lovers. These thoughts sent Montriveau flying from Cadiz to Marseilles, and from Marseilles to Paris.

A few months after his return to France, a merchant brig, fitted out and munitioned for active service, set sail from the port of Marseilles for Spain. The vessel had been chartered by several distinguished men, most of them Frenchmen, who, smitten with a romantic passion for the East, wished to make a journey to those lands. Montriveau's familiar knowledge of Eastern customs made him an invaluable travelling companion, and at the entreaty of the rest he had joined the expedition; the Minister of War appointed him lieutenant-general, and put him on the Artillery Commission to facilitate his departure.

Twenty-fours hours later the brig lay to off the north-west shore of an island within sight of the Spanish coast. She had been specially chosen for her shallow keel and light mastage, so that she might lie at anchor in safety half a league away from the reefs that secure the island from approach in this direction. If fishing vessels or the people on the island caught sight of the brig, they were scarcely likely to feel suspicious of her at once; and besides, it was easy to give a reason for her presence without delay. Montriveau hoisted the flag of the United States before they came in sight of the island, and the crew of the vessel were all American sailors, who spoke nothing but English. One of M. de Montriveau's companions took the men ashore in the ship's longboat, and made them so drunk at an inn in the little town that they could not talk. Then he gave out that the brig was manned by treasure-seekers, a gang of men whose hobby was well known in the United States; indeed, some Spanish writer had written a history of them. The presence of the brig among the reefs was now sufficiently explained. The owners of the vessel, according to the self-styled boatswain's mate, were looking for the wreck of a galleon which foundered thereabouts in 1778 with a cargo of treasure from Mexico. The people at the inn and the authorities asked no more questions.

Armand, and the devoted friends who were helping him in his difficult enterprise, were all from the first of the opinion that there was no hope of rescuing or carrying off Sister Theresa by force or stratagem from the side of the little town. Wherefore these bold spirits, with one accord, determined to take the bull by the horns. They would make a way to the convent at the most seemingly inaccessible point; like General Lamarque, at the storming of Capri, they would conquer Nature. The cliff at the end of the island, a sheer block of granite, afforded even less hold than the rock of Capri. So it seemed at least to Montriveau, who had taken part in that incredible exploit, while the nuns in his eyes were much more redoubtable than Sir Hudson Lowe. To raise a hubbub over carrying off the Duchess would cover them with confusion. They might as well set siege to the town and convent, like pirates, and leave not a single soul to tell of their victory. So for them their expedition wore but two aspects. There should be a conflagration and a feat of arms that should dismay all Europe, while the motives of the crime remained unknown; or, on the other hand, a mysterious, aerial descent which should persuade the nuns that the Devil himself had paid them a visit. They had decided upon the latter course in the secret council held before they left Paris, and subsequently everything had been done to insure the success of an expedition which promised some real excitement to jaded spirits weary of Paris and its pleasures.

An extremely light pirogue, made at Marseilles on a Malayan model, enabled them to cross the reef, until the rocks rose from out of the water. Then two cables of iron wire were fastened several feet apart between one rock and another. These wire ropes slanted upwards and downwards in opposite directions, so that baskets of iron wire could travel to and fro along them; and in this manner the rocks were covered with a system of baskets and wire-cables, not unlike the filaments which a certain species of spider weaves about a tree. The Chinese, an essentially imitative people, were the first to take a lesson from the work of instinct. Fragile as these bridges were, they were always ready for use; high waves and the caprices of the sea could not throw them out of working order; the ropes hung just sufficiently slack, so as to present to the breakers that particular curve discovered by Cachin, the immortal creator of the harbour at Cherbourg. Against this cunningly devised line the angry surge is powerless; the law of that curve was a secret wrested from Nature by that faculty of observation in which nearly all human genius consists.

M. de Montriveau's companions were alone on board the vessel, and out of sight of every human eye. No one from the deck of a passing vessel could have discovered either the brig hidden among the reefs, or the men at work among the rocks; they lay below the ordinary range of the most powerful telescope. Eleven days were spent in preparation, before the Thirteen, with all their infernal power, could reach the foot of the cliffs. The body of the rock rose up straight from the sea to a height of thirty fathoms. Any attempt to climb the sheer wall of granite seemed impossible; a mouse might as well try to creep up the slippery sides of a plain china vase. Still there was a cleft, a straight line of fissure so fortunately placed that large blocks of wood could be wedged firmly into it at a distance of about a foot apart. Into these blocks the daring workers drove iron cramps, specially made for the purpose, with a broad iron bracket at the outer end, through which a hole had been drilled. Each bracket carried a light deal board which corresponded with a notch made in a pole that reached to the top of the cliffs, and was firmly planted in the beach at their feet. With ingenuity worthy of these men who found nothing impossible, one of their number, a skilled mathematician, had calculated the angle from which the steps must start; so that from the middle they rose gradually, like the sticks of a fan, to the top of the cliff, and descended in the same fashion to its base. That miraculously light, yet perfectly firm, staircase cost them twenty-two days of toil. A little tinder and the surf of the sea would destroy all trace of it forever in a single night. A betrayal of the secret was impossible; and all search for the violators of the convent was doomed to failure.

At the top of the rock there was a platform with sheer precipice on all sides. The Thirteen, reconnoitring the ground with their glasses from the masthead, made certain that though the ascent was steep and rough, there would be no difficulty in gaining the convent garden, where the trees were thick enough for a hiding-place. After such great efforts they would not risk the success of their enterprise, and were compelled to wait till the moon passed out of her last quarter.

For two nights Montriveau, wrapped in his cloak, lay out on the rock platform. The singing at vespers and matins filled him with unutterable joy. He stood under the wall to hear the music of the organ, listening intently for one voice among the rest. But in spite of the silence, the confused effect of music was all that reached his ears. In those sweet harmonies defects of execution are lost; the pure spirit of art comes into direct communication with the spirit of the hearer, making no demand on the attention, no strain on the power of listening. Intolerable memories awoke. All the love within him seemed to break into blossom again at the breath of that music; he tried to find auguries of happiness in the air. During the last night he sat with his eyes fixed upon an ungrated window, for bars were not needed on the side of the precipice. A light shone there all through the hours; and that instinct of the heart, which is sometimes true, and as often false, cried within him, "She is there!"

"She is certainly there! Tomorrow she will be mine," he said to himself, and joy blended with the slow tinkling of a bell that began to ring.

Strange unaccountable workings of the heart! The nun, wasted by yearning love, worn out with tears and fasting, prayer and vigils; the woman of nine-and-twenty, who had passed through heavy trials, was loved more passionately than the lighthearted girl, the woman of four-and-twenty, the sylphide, had ever been. But is there not, for men of vigorous character, something attractive in the sublime expression engraven on women's faces by the impetuous stirrings of thought and misfortunes of no ignoble kind? Is there not a beauty of suffering which is the most interesting of all beauty to those men who feel that within them there is an inexhaustible wealth of tenderness and consoling pity for a creature so gracious in weakness, so strong with love? It is the ordinary nature that is attracted by young, smooth, pink-and-white beauty, or, in one word, by prettiness. In some faces love awakens amid the wrinkles carved by sorrow and the ruin made by melancholy; Montriveau could not but feel drawn to these. For cannot a lover, with the voice of a great longing, call forth a wholly new creature? a creature athrob with the life but just begun breaks forth for him alone, from the outward form that is fair for him, and faded for all the world besides. Does he not love two women?—One of them, as others see her, is pale and wan and sad; but the other, the unseen love that his heart knows, is an angel who understands life through feeling, and is adorned in all her glory only for love's high festivals.

The General left his post before sunrise, but not before he had heard voices singing together, sweet voices full of tenderness sounding faintly from the cell. When he came down to the foot of the cliffs where his friends were waiting, he told them that never in his life had he felt such enthralling bliss, and in the few words there was that unmistakable thrill of repressed strong feeling, that magnificent utterance which all men respect.

That night eleven of his devoted comrades made the ascent in the darkness. Each man carried a poniard, a provision of chocolate, and a set of house-breaking tools. They climbed the outer walls with scaling-ladders, and crossed the cemetery of the convent. Montriveau recognised the long, vaulted gallery through which he went to the parlour, and remembered the windows of the room. His plans were made and adopted in a moment. They would effect an entrance through one of the windows in the Carmelite's half of the parlour, find their way along the corridors, ascertain whether the sister's names were written on the doors, find Sister Theresa's cell, surprise her as she slept, and carry her off, bound and gagged. The programme presented no difficulties to men who combined boldness and a convict's dexterity with the knowledge peculiar to men of the world, especially as they would not scruple to give a stab to ensure silence.

In two hours the bars were sawn through. Three men stood on guard outside, and two inside the parlour. The rest, barefooted, took up their posts along the corridor. Young Henri de Marsay, the most dexterous man among them, disguised by way of precaution in a Carmelite's robe, exactly like the costume of the convent, led the way, and Montriveau came immediately behind him. The clock struck three just as the two men reached the dormitory cells. They soon saw the position. Everything was perfectly quiet. With the help of a dark lantern they read the names luckily written on every door, together with the picture of a saint or saints and the mystical words which every nun takes as a kind of motto for the beginning of her new life and the revelation of her last thought. Montriveau reached Sister Theresa's door and read the inscription, *Sub invocatione sanctae matris Theresae*, and her motto, *Adoremus in aeternum*. Suddenly his companion laid a hand on his shoulder. A bright light was streaming through the chinks of the door. M. de Ronquerolles came up at that moment.

"All the nuns are in the church," he said; "they are beginning the Office for the Dead."

"I will stay here," said Montriveau. "Go back into the parlour, and shut the door at the end of the passage."

He threw open the door and rushed in, preceded by his disguised companion, who let down the veil over his face.

There before them lay the dead Duchess; her plank bed had been laid on the floor of the outer room of her cell, between two lighted candles. Neither Montriveau nor de Marsay spoke a word or uttered a cry; but they looked into each other's faces. The General's dumb gesture tried to say, "Let us carry her away!"

"Quickly" shouted Ronquerolles, "the procession of nuns is leaving the church. You will be caught!"

With magical swiftness of movement, prompted by an intense desire, the dead woman was carried into the convent parlour, passed through the window, and lowered from the walls before the Abbess, followed by the nuns, returned to take up Sister Theresa's body. The sister left in charge had imprudently left her post; there were secrets that she longed to know; and so busy was she ransacking the inner room, that she heard nothing, and was horrified when she came back to find that the body was gone. Before the women, in their blank amazement, could think of making a search, the Duchess had been lowered by a cord to the foot of the crags, and Montriveau's companions had destroyed all traces of their work. By nine o'clock that morning there was not a sign to show that either staircase or wire-cables had ever existed, and Sister Theresa's body had been taken on board. The brig came into the port to ship her crew, and sailed that day.

Montriveau, down in the cabin, was left alone with Antoinette de Navarreins. For some hours it seemed as if her dead face was transfigured for him by that unearthly beauty which the calm of death gives to the body before it perishes.

"Look here," said Ronquerolles when Montriveau reappeared on deck, "*that* was a woman once, now it is nothing. Let us tie a cannon ball to both feet and throw the body overboard; and if ever you think of her again, think of her as of some book that you read as a boy."

"Yes," assented Montriveau, "it is nothing now but a dream."

"That is sensible of you. Now, after this, have passions; but as for love, a man ought to know how to place it wisely; it is only a woman's last love that can satisfy a man's first love."

ADDENDUM

Note: The Duchesse de Langeais is the second part of a trilogy. Part one is entitled Ferragus and part three is The Girl with the Golden Eyes. In other addendum references all three stories are usually combined under the title The Thirteen.

The following personages appear in other stories of the Human Comedy.

Blamont-Chauvry, Princesse de
  Madame Firmiani
  The Lily of the Valley

Grandlieu, Duc Ferdinand de
  The Gondreville Mystery
  A Bachelor's Establishment
  Modeste Mignon
  Scenes from a Courtesan's Life

Granville, Comtesse Angelique de
  A Second Home
  A Daughter of Eve

Keller, Madame Francois
  Domestic Peace
  The Member for Arcis

Langeais, Duc de
  An Episode under the Terror

Langeais, Duchesse Antoinette de
  Father Goriot
  Ferragus

Marsay, Henri de
  Ferragus
  The Girl with the Golden Eyes
  The Unconscious Humorists

Another Study of Woman
The Lily of the Valley
Father Goriot
Jealousies of a Country Town
Ursule Mirouet
A Marriage Settlement
Lost Illusions
A Distinguished Provincial at Paris
Letters of Two Brides
The Ball at Sceaux
Modeste Mignon
The Secrets of a Princess
The Gondreville Mystery
A Daughter of Eve

Montriveau, General Marquis Armand de
Father Goriot
Lost Illusions
A Distinguished Provincial at Paris
Another Study of Woman
Pierrette
The Member for Arcis

Navarreins, Duc de
A Bachelor's Establishment
Colonel Chabert
The Muse of the Department
Jealousies of a Country Town
The Peasantry
Scenes from a Courtesan's Life
The Country Parson
The Magic Skin
The Gondreville Mystery
The Secrets of a Princess
Cousin Betty

Pamiers, Vidame de
Ferragus

Jealousies of a Country Town

Ronquerolles, Marquis de
  The Imaginary Mistress
  The Peasantry
  Ursule Mirouet
  A Woman of Thirty
  Another Study of Woman
  Ferragus
  The Girl with the Golden Eyes
  The Member for Arcis

Serizy, Comtesse de
  A Start in Life
  Ferragus
  Ursule Mirouet
  A Woman of Thirty
  Scenes from a Courtesan's Life
  Another Study of Woman
  The Imaginary Mistress

Soulanges, Comtesse Hortense de
  Domestic Peace
  The Peasantry

Talleyrand-Perigord, Charles-Maurice de
  The Chouans
  The Gondreville Mystery
  Letters of Two Brides
  Gaudissart II

CPSIA information can be obtained
at www.ICGtesting.com
Printed in the USA
BVHW031041040423
661729BV00013B/892